Also by Emily Stone

Spare Me

Hansel and Greta

The Accident

a novel

Emily Stone

This is a work of fiction. Names, characters, places, and incidents are products of the author's imagination or are used fictitiously. Any resemblance to actual events, locales, or persons, living or dead, is entirely coincidental.

Copyright © 2015 by Emily Stone

Cover photograph copyright © 2014 by Emily Stone

All rights reserved.

ISBN-13: 978-1506104485

ISBN-10: 1506104487

Printed by CreateSpace, a division of Amazon

For more information on other titles by Emily Stone,

visit emilystonebooks.com

For Gavin and Fiona

THE ACCIDENT

One of us will be the one who dies too young.
One of us will be the one who loses a best friend.
One of us will be the one who loses all memory.
One of us will be the one who tells the story.

PREFACE

There was no deafening crunch of shattered glass as their bodies propelled through a windshield. There was no rainbow of glittering crystal shards, flying, like double tornadoes sent on a mission to heaven and hell. There was no pit-pattering of broken glass on the dirt parking lot like a sudden hailstorm as their bodies fell to earth.

There was no windshield to break.

There were no airbags exploding into action to cushion young, malleable brains. There were no seat belts fastened around their waists to hold them back like a mother's loving arm. There were no things to save them except themselves.

Bam.

There was a baby-blue Land Rover hitting a rock with a thudding crash.

And then.

There was silence.

There were two boys ejected from their seats.

There were two boys forever connected in the air, floating silently for just a second, together.

There were two boys flying over the hood of a vehicle, instantly catapulted toward an unknowable future.

And there was one witness to it all.

30 MINUTES BEFORE THE ACCIDENT

Before the accident happened, I never could have imagined my summer would end the way it did. I was just an eighteen-year-old girl in a red patterned sun dress, my long brown hair falling in layered waves, hiding the secrets of summer that trailed across my face like freckles brought out by the sun.

If I could have rewound time and gone back seven weeks, I would have changed some of the choices I made. Maybe I wouldn't have let Luke in the sliding glass doors that first day. Maybe I wouldn't have let him into my heart. But mostly, I wouldn't have gotten into that Land Rover.

It was late summer when my story ended, and the fading heat of August was upon the small beach town of Mattamuskee, Rhode Island.

I was in a ranch-style house with about thirty other girls and guys who were talking so loud they were drowning out the music that came from tiny speakers in the corners of the ceiling.

Cigarette smoke blew around someone's parents' china closet with ugly little Hummel dolls in it.

Luke, where are you? I thought.

Again.

"April, this is the *besht* college party I've ever been to," my friend Steph slurred as we sat on a light brown leather couch with red plastic beer cups in hand. "Luke is *aweshum*. I take back everything I said before." She shook her blond curls like she was releasing all the bad karma that Luke and I had started.

I rolled my eyes and said, "This is the *only* college party you've ever been to. And you've never taken back anything you've said before, so I'll ask you tomorrow when you're sober."

A spray of piss-yellow beer jumped out of her cup and landed on the couch. This was not how I pictured Luke's great send-off. Or the end of my one extraordinary summer.

It had all sped by so fast.

Just that day, before we landed at the ranch-house kegger, Steph and I had sat in beach chairs for hours at Crescent Beach, catching up. We had been apart the whole summer, so we'd spent the day marathon-talking—both of us racing to get the most mileage in. My nanny job had been amazing. Hunter and his baby sister Rosy were the world's greatest kids. And on top of that, I'd fallen hardcore for Luke, despite a complicated web of "innocent" lies that surrounded the whole me-and-him thing.

Didn't we all do stupid things for love? Nothing *bad* had happened.

Now, sitting next to Steph on the couch, with my thighs sticking to the couch pleather, all Steph's scoldings about sneaking around with Luke and jeopardizing my job were long forgotten in the bottom of her plastic beer cup. Now Steph was drunk with a capital D, and, while it wasn't the first time, it wasn't really her all-the-time style. Or mine. I pulled on the hem of my red-patterned sundress and tried to unstick my thighs from the couch suction.

"Look at that guy Ollie over there," she said. "That guy is waaasted."

We watched Ollie, Luke's friend that he picked up on the way there, take funnel after funnel of beer to the hoots and hollers of his guy friends. His largeness included a booming voice and relentless high fives. His light curly brown hair was cut close to his scalp and he wore a gaudy green polo. He was the stereotypical drunkio we'd seen in silly college movies, who everyone loved but no one could handle. That night at the party, Luke, for some reason, was loving Ollie's jokes and hand gestures. I even saw him pour one of the beers down the funnel that traveled into Ollie's mouth at megaspeed.

"Well, I think I am going to sequester myself into the school library next year until everyone gets the whole partying thing out of their system," I said. I flicked a little salmon-colored nail polish off my nail and shook my long brown hair in front of my face.

"Great idea," Steph joked. "I'm sure those are the only two *oppshuns* in college. Keg parties or library cubbies. I'm *shuure* there's not a single other activity going on." She pinched me.

"Okay, you're right," I said, rolling my eyes.

Steph leaned her head in. "Good . . . you're right. . . . I love you."

She laughed as we bumped heads.

I had my eye on Luke again, so I could relax. He was talking to a group of guys. Luke, all tan, with his free hand jammed into his jeans' back pocket, and brown medium-length hair full of natural summer sun. My crush was still alive.

Steph tried to stifle a laugh but it came out like a snort as I discreetly pointed across the room at the couple I thought would be putting on a PDA show, for sure. Steph eyed the gymnast girl with capri pants who had been flirting like mad with the cute guy wearing a T-shirt that said *Problem Child*.

"So far, nothing," I said. "But watch. Some girl always loses her cool at parties like these."

Luke came by to check on us. Since he was the designated driver, he assured me that he wasn't getting drunk. He showed me the water he was drinking in between beers. I wanted to offer to drive, since I was definitely *not* drunk, but I knew he would never let me drive his precious, baby blue, vintage 1967 Land Rover.

"Luke, you *mush* be peeing like a racehorse!" Steph blurted out, her eyes wide at his double-fisted drinks—water in one hand, keg beer in the other.

Luke smiled at her and nodded. "Oh yeah. Drink like a fish much?"

Steph slapped her leg and fell to her knees laughing. Luke moved on. Oh God.

"Would you like a water?" I said to Steph.

She mimicked me, getting up, "Would you like a water?" She wasn't being mean, she was just being Steph. On Heineken.

I pulled the edge of her miniskirt down and said, "Maybe you should slow down."

She covered her mouth like she had been caught being bad and said, "Yes, Mom. You are correct, Mom." She giggled into her cup.

Good God. Getting her and Ollie into the Land Rover later was going to be a feat.

I crowd-watched a pretty girl with waist-length red hair leaning up against a door frame. Ollie, in gaudy green, sidled up to her and said, "You holding that wall up?" The girl looked at him confused, then looked at the door frame, then slowly looked back at him. For a second I think she *did* think she was holding the wall up. Ollie laughed and joined a circle of guys who were trying for good posture by holding their cups in front of their stomachs with their free hands strategically resting in their front pockets. Ollie was like a big octopus in their circle, all arms and elbows moving while he talked, laughed, and missed the cues that he was one step beyond everyone else.

I got up and followed the direction Luke had gone. I spotted him talking to some guy with a lip ring in the kitchen, right next to the big silver keg. I couldn't see what was in Luke's water cup anymore.

Luke and I made eye contact. I was trying to say "I'm bored," "Can we go?" with my eyes, but all I got back were eyes from Luke that seemed to say, "Hey, 'sup." And then he kept talking with his friend. I splashed the rest of my beer down my throat and put the plastic cup on an end table.

I looked around to check on Steph and saw that my best friend—who had just, minutes before, been commenting about the drunken octopus in a lime green polo that infiltrated every circle—was sucking face with him on the couch. My jaw dropped open when I saw Steph's knee curled around Ollie's leg and her body turned into him while her other hand held her beer cup away from her body. Oh my God. Total PDA.

Ollie had his hand circling around Steph's waist and was rubbing the skin under her shirt. I actually saw her tongue dart out and search for his mouth. I strode over and jostled my bag next to her, but they kept on making out like they were in the back of some old-school station wagon. I dropped my bag on the floor and cleared my throat.

"I'm going to go get a water," I said. "Do you want one?"

Steph waved me off with the fingers that loosely gripped her cup.

"I'll be right back," I said. She nodded and rubbed herself up against Ollie.

Better here than during her first week of college, I guess.

I strode into the kitchen, where Luke was still talking to that guy. He smiled when he saw me and stretched out an arm. He wrapped it around my shoulder as I got closer and said, "April, this is Trent."

Trent shot his hand out of his cool-guy front pocket and I shook it. "Sweet," he said. "You work together?"

I nodded.

Luke released me and made quotation marks with his fingers. "Yeah, we 'work' together!" he said. They both cracked up and did a fist bump.

I rolled my eyes and turned to the keg.

"Oh, naw, naw, don't be like that, baby," Luke said, putting on some homeboy voice he picked up off TV. "We just playin'. We just playin'."

Trent took my annoyed face as his cue to leave, so I tried to think of something to say to Luke as I filled my cup with more yellow beer. The tap on the keg was slow and the beer trickled out.

"Here, hold it down lower," Luke said, taking the tap from my hand and bringing my cup down to the side of the silver keg.

"You would know," I said, crossing my arms across my chest.

Luke stood up when the cup was full. He gave me the

puppy eyes. "Are you mad?" he asked.

"About what?"

"I don't know. Girls always get mad at parties." Luke scratched his shoulder.

"I'm not 'girls.'" I held my hand out for the cup. He passed it to me. "And yeah, I'm a little mad. *We 'work' together?* Do you think that makes you look cool or something? How do you think that makes me feel?"

Luke shrugged.

"You're just acting so different," I said. Was he drunk or did he just act different around his friends?

"So are you," he said, leaning to pick something off his shoe.

"What the?" I said, totally confused.

"April, what's the worst thing you've ever done?" Luke asked. "Come on, fess up, *what's the worst thing you've ever done?*"

Luke was giving me apologetic love eyes.

"What are you talking about, Luke? What do you mean?" It was hard to stay mad when he was so close.

"What are you really upset about?" he prodded.

I thought for a second. I guess I was just nervous about him leaving in a few days. And me going back to life before Luke. And not knowing what would come after.

Not even thirty minutes after.

Luke took my hand and we walked through the living room. Ollie and Steph were still on the couch going at it. Now they had a few observers who were egging them on. A small group in the corner was actually chanting "Hickey, hickey, hickey," like this was seventh grade.

Luke looked at them, then at me, and shook his head. "Chug it," he said.

"What?"

He was pointing at the beer he had just filled up for

me.

"Chug it," he repeated.

"I can't chug a beer. I've never chugged a beer in my life." It wasn't a priss statement, just a matter of facts.

He held up his own cup and said, "Watch." Then he tilted the cup up to his lips and let it gush down his throat in big gulps. Super-unattractive. So far, two strikes, Luke. Was he the same guy I had fallen for during those fleeting weeks of summer? He had to be in there somewhere.

When Luke finished chugging, he raised his cup up and burped. Loudly.

"I am definitely not going to burp," I said.

He fisted his chest. "Makes you feel better." Then he kissed me on the cheek. "Now chug it. I want to show you something outside."

Nothing was making any sense. Were we ever going home?

I shook my head. I was about to chug my first beer while Steph worked toward her first one-night-stand with a college guy.

It wasn't a pretty sight. Beer ran down my chin and over both sides of my face as I tried to swallow the drink in ten seconds. I could feel it going down like a dam had burst and not one second of it felt natural. I was actively going against nature and everything my body wanted me to do.

I pulled the empty cup away and wiggled my head around. I wiped my face with my hands and looked at Luke. "You were saying?"

He smiled and took my elbow, leading me to the front yard. The noises of the party were muted out on the grass. We sat down and Luke said, "Check it out. It's my favorite moon."

The sky was bright with a crooked almost-half moon. "What kind of moon is that?" I asked.

"I don't know." Luke burped again. Quietly, this time into his hand.

"It's your favorite moon and you don't even know what it's called? Is it a half moon or a crescent? Or something else entirely?" The moon hung there like a reminder of eternity.

"April, do you have to take everything so literally? I just love this moon. It's my favorite because the first time I've seen it is with you."

The first time he'd seen this type of moon was with me? What kind of line was that?

"Are you drunk?" I said.

He laughed. "Are you?"

"Here, maybe this will help: Do we *work together*? Or are you just working *me*?" My words were coming out of some devilish place I wasn't used to accessing.

Luke stood up, amused. At least he wasn't angry. "Maybe this will help." He cupped his hands over his mouth to make a megaphone. "NO. We don't work together. BUT . . . I . . . LOVE . . . YOU."

"Okay, sit down," I said.

He shook his head. "Should I repeat myself?" he said. "I don't think my dad and Cynthia heard me yet." I imagined my nanny job just a few miles down the road. I pictured Doug and Cynthia Rogers, the parents, tucked into a late-night movie in bed while the kids slept down the hall.

"Oh, no, that's quite all right." I stood up to face him. I put my arms around his neck and pulled him to me. I was ready to stop picking fights with him. I wanted to tell him that, yeah, I kinda-sorta loved him, too. That maybe I would consider the long-distance thing once we went to school. I kissed his neck and breathed in the sweet smell of him. I ran my tongue up to his earlobe and stopped when he started to shiver. "I love you, too, okay?" I whispered into his neck.

He laughed. "Are you sure? Because I can't really hear you and —"

I cut him off by kissing him full on the mouth. Right there on the front lawn. With his hands jammed into the back pockets of my jeans. My hips jammed into his. We kissed like it was hello and good-bye all in one.

Luke and I were the second blatant act of PDA at the party.

The two eighteen-year-olds making a splash.

Oh well. What happens in Mattamuskee stays in Mattamuskee.

Except when it doesn't.

Luke and I were ripped apart from our embrace by the sound of his 1967 Land Rover starting up. We let go of each other to see it being slowly backed down the driveway, then idling by the street. Luke immediately broke into a run, yelling, "Ollie, wait!"

I glanced back at the party, then started running, too.

Ollie turned around and looked over his shoulder as we approached. Luke's old baby-blue Land Rover was kind of like a Jeep because it didn't have a hard top. But it didn't have those supporting bars around it like Jeeps did. The thing was, Luke's Rover didn't even have a *windshield*. Luke never, ever had the windshield up. It was more like half a vehicle. It was made for driving on the beach and safaris and stuff, but we had never actually driven it on the beach.

"Whassup, guys?" Ollie drawled from the driver's seat. His lime green tennis shirt had a big wet stain on the front.

Luke tried to keep his cool.

"What are you doing, man?"

Ollie's hand was on the gear shift. "Climb in," Ollie said. "I'm just waiting for Stace."

Luke was at the driver-side door. "Dude, gimme the keys. This is my ride, remember?"

Ollie pushed him back. "I just gotta run to the store and back. You don't even need to be bothered. Go back to your lady." He pointed at me and smiled.

Steph came weaving down the front lawn, her espadrilles in hand, and opened the passenger-side door. She climbed in and leaned her head back on the seat.

"Stace," Ollie said, giving her a kiss.

"*Steph*," I corrected.

"Das what I said." Then before Luke could strong-arm him out of the car, Ollie hit the gas and headed out onto the street.

"Dammit!" Luke said, hitting his legs with his hands.

We watched as Luke's Land Rover sped to the stop sign, came to a short stop, then paused for a second too long. We stood at the end of the driveway watching as Ollie took a right without using a turn signal and the red taillights sped out of sight.

"Do something!" I said. "My best friend is in that car!"

Luke ran his hand through his hair and shook his face so it made a monster sound. "Why the hell did I give him my keys?" he said.

"What?" I shrieked.

Luke started heading up the driveway. "Come on, get your stuff. We've gotta hijack the car when he gets back."

"What are you talking about?"

Luke ignored me.

"Why did you give him your keys?" I grabbed his elbow and looked him in the eye. "Don't you think you should call the police? He's drunk!"

Luke spun around and released his elbow. "Are you

crazy? The store is two blocks away. He'll be right back. I gave him the keys hours ago, when he wasn't so lit. Then I forgot, okay? Sue me."

I ignored his attitude and tried to focus on the situation at hand.

"Look, what if he isn't going to the store? Did you see how drunk Steph was? What if he tries to rape her? What if he gets lost? What if –"

Luke cut me off as we approached the house. "Get your bag. He's not going to rape her. He's not that kind of guy. Look, he's not even *that drunk*. Did you see how big he is? He can handle a lot more than the rest of us."

We walked inside the house to see the party still raging. Luke pointed to my bag and picked up his long-sleeve plaid shirt off the couch. As he was putting it on, I said. "Just call the cops and report him. That way no one gets hurt."

Luke looked out the living room's bay window. "Right. Call the cops and no one gets hurt. My car gets impounded. Ollie gets a DWI. The party gets busted. You and Steph get busted for underage drinking. My brother and sister have no nanny. Great idea, April."

My head was spinning. None of that mattered if it saved Steph from having to relive a night from hell. What if he had sex with her and she was too drunk to do anything about it? That was still rape. I just kept picturing the way Ollie said "Stace" and then hit the gas like it was a bumper car.

I pulled out my cell and quickly texted Steph:

GET OUT @ store. Meet me there.

"What are you doing?" Luke said angrily as I hit Send.

"If you don't call the cops, I will," I said, starting to press 9.

The Accident

Our conversation had been picked up by some of the partygoers, and a guy butted in, "Why is she calling the po-po?" His friend swiped the phone out of my hand and closed it. They got up in Luke's face and tried to start with him.

"Dude, outside, outside," Luke said, backing away from them with his hands up. His plaid shirt was waving in the breeze from the open front door. "She's not going to call the cops." He gave me a withering look, and the two guys and I followed him outside.

Hearing the word cops, more kids came outside. Luke held his hand out to the guys who had my phone. "No lies," he said. "She's not dialing 911. Not under my watch. You know how chics get."

The guys handed Luke my phone and did some high fives.

I was ready to go off on a tirade about the crazy-bad way guys at parties talk about girls. But Luke was pleading me with his eyes to chill.

I couldn't. I looked at the two guys. "Ollie took Luke's car. With my best friend in it. Yeah. So I am kind of freaking out. Can you blame me?"

Luke gave me eyes of death and put the phone in his front pocket. I slung my bag over my arm and waited for the guys to respond.

One laughed while the other one covered his mouth, crouching down and saying, "Dog, dog. . ."

Then the first one said, "All Ollie wants is more beer, not booty. The only one he's going to hurt is himself, dog. He'll be wrapped around the porcelain goddess tomorrow morning!" The guys broke up in laughter. Even Luke cracked a smile as I stood there.

So everyone except me thought this big, strong guy—stronger than Steph—driving someone else's vehicle around dark roads was harmless. Un-freaking-believable.

Luke winked at me and put his finger up to say he'd be right back. Before I could protest he was jogging back into the house. Filling up another plastic cup? At this point, I wouldn't have been surprised if he had started smoking a crackpipe. I stood on the lawn and folded my arms over my chest. This. Freaking. Sucked. A couple of guys were watching me.

"What are you looking at?" I barked.

They shrugged their shoulders and went inside for a refill. I watched as they went back into the house. Through the bay window next to the front door, they walked past Luke, giving him a back slap. Luke was talking to a kid in a camo T-shirt. I stood there watching, waiting, wondering when I would get my phone back. The kid in the camo shirt was making these hand gestures, as if he was trying to calm Luke down.

As I stood there on the lawn alone, I realized that nothing was under my control anymore. A ton of the partyers were talking about Ollie taking Luke's car. I heard one girl come outside, saying, "I saw her when she was in the bathroom, but then she got into the car with *him*." Another girl groaned. "Ugh. I wish I had stopped her. But all she asked for was fresh air."

Down the street, I heard the familiar sound of the Land Rover's engine.

"Oh, God," I said, clutching my heart. I breathed out as I saw the Land Rover coming our way. I didn't know if this was good or bad, but I made a mental thank-you to whoever was watching over Steph.

"Luke!" I yelled into the house. He came running outside.

The moon was right above us—Crescent Beach and the safety of the Rogers' house so near. I pictured Rosy and

The Accident

Hunter sleeping soundly in their kid-size beds. I wished I was back there under my own lavender duvet with the glowing colors of the baby monitor. Maybe we could rewrite this night.

Soon. Soon.

Ollie used his turn signal to pull into the driveway, and he cranked the vehicle onto the grass. He pulled to a stop and we ran to the side of the Rover.

"Where's Steph?" I said, alarmed to not see her cascade of curls in the passenger seat.

Ollie thumbed to the backseat. "She hurled and then she passed out."

Luke walked slowly to the vehicle, trying to maintain his cool. "Get out of the car. Give me the keys. Now!" he shouted at Ollie.

I ran around the car, noticing a fresh spray of puke on the outside of the passenger-side door. Steph was lying down in the backseat. I did not use the door, but instead I hopped over the side and got next to her in the seat.

Ollie kept his hands on the keys in the ignition and motioned to Luke. "Get in. You're in no *shtate* to drive."

"Get the hell out of that seat!" Luke roared, coming at Ollie from the passenger-side door.

I shook Steph and she groaned.

"Come on, Steph," I said, wishing Luke had wrestled the keys back from Ollie by now. "I've got to get you out of here."

"Leave me alone," she said. "I go home." Her shirt had vomit on it so I pulled a baby wipe out of my bag and blotted it off. She rolled onto her side so I was able to clean the gunk out of her hair and wipe her face. I put the soiled baby wipes on the floor of the car and looked at Luke.

Luke had opened the passenger-side door and had one foot in the car as he negotiated with Ollie. Ollie wouldn't budge from the driver's seat.

"Man, go get your shirt from inside and then we'll take off," Luke tried, pretending he wasn't mad anymore.

Ollie just swayed his head around like it had a loose bolt. "Man, I told you. I didn't bring a shirt. Just hop in and we'll go to the next packie."

I pulled Steph's legs onto the floor of the Rover and extracted the seat belt from underneath her. I gave Luke a pleading look. Apparently the package store they went to was closed and there was another one a few miles away.

"Ollie, dude. You can drive my car all day tomorrow," he said, his voice staying level. "On the backroads, all right? But, man, you're not on my insurance. If we get pulled over right now, I'm screwed." It was like he had erased his anger from two seconds ago with a determined, focused calm.

Not to mention that the Rover had its top off and its windshield was tucked down inside the front of the vehicle. If any car driving down the street with four young people looked suspicious, it was this one. I succeeded in buckling in Steph, although she fought me when I had to reach under her boobs to get the seat belt snapped. "Ow," she cried, then closed her eyes again and breathed out through her mouth.

"Ollie," I said. "Let Luke take us home. Look, I've buckled Steph in."

"Dude, get in the freakin' car," Ollie said to Luke. "You drive like a moron after a few beers," Ollie said. "I've got master skills in that department. Come on. You'll be thanking me for this later."

Luke reached over to pull the keys away, but Ollie's hand intercepted. Ollie turned the key in the ignition. I heard a small crowd from the party chanting, "Go, Ollie. Go, Ollie." I turned to look at them in amazement, and as I did, my head was whipped back as the Rover lunged up the front lawn and veered toward the house. Luke was hanging on with one leg flying out of the passenger-side door that was still open.

Ollie revved the engine and sent the Land Rover up the front lawn and headed toward the crowd. Luke pulled his leg in and tried to close the door.

"You crazy mofo!" a girl shouted.

"Get out of the way!" another kid said. The kids went scrambling into the house, but at the last moment, Ollie cut the wheel and drove down the walkway that connected to the driveway. Luke was still standing up, trying to get his balance as he held on to his seat and the door that kept swinging out. His plaid shirt waved like a mercy flag.

"Pull the *F* over!" Luke screamed.

But Ollie drove the vehicle down onto the driveway and pulled out onto the street without stopping. The sharp left that he took forced Luke's door to close and Luke fell into the passenger seat. Luke was writhing with anger as Ollie played the game of keep away—keeping Luke away from the gear shift, the ignition, the steering wheel.

My bag was in between me and Steph, and I felt all around the seat for my seat belt. I found one end, but the piece that it needed to clip into was missing. I shoved my bag to the floor and dug around under Steph.

"Where are you, where are you, where are you?" I cried.

"Stop it," Steph whined, moving around.

Then I felt something hard. I pulled the buckle piece out and connected it to my lap belt. I sighed with relief and sat back in my seat only to be quickly jarred right and left. I screamed, my voice coming out without warning. Ollie and Luke were fighting over the steering wheel.

"Get your hands off, you ninja warrior!" Ollie was saying in a maniacal way. It was like he was playing a video game.

"Pull over!" Luke yelled at him.

Ollie slammed the turn signal up and barreled to the right, turning down a different street and out of view of the party. Luke and Ollie continued to argue, shouting at each other while Luke tried to wrest control. We turned off the residential streets and were on a side-cut street that was bordered by swamps.

"April! Don't!" Luke yelled at me although I wasn't doing anything. I was just sitting there holding on to the seat for dear life.

But it was his trick.

In the split second that Ollie checked the rearview mirror to see what I was "doing," Luke reached over to the keys, quickly turned them, and pulled them out of the ignition.

"Oh, you bloody wanker," Ollie said in a bad English accent as the Rover started to tremble. He put it in nuetral and the Rover started slowing down as we coasted on the flat road. Ollie weaved the steering wheel back and forth lazily, making a video-game sound with his voice.

"Waa waa. Game over," he said robotically. Ollie turned and smiled at Luke. "You win."

"This isn't *F-ing* funny!" Luke said, opening his door and hopping out. He slammed it shut. "Now get the heck out!"

Ollie laughed a deep belly laugh and opened his door. He put one leg out of the car and mimicked Luke, "F-ing funny. Get the *heck* out!" he laughed. "What, are we in the Bible Belt?"

I watched as Ollie walked around the front of the car and Luke walked around the back.

Ollie held his hands up like the police were there.

"Never mind. Never you mind," Ollie said slowly. "I

get it. Game over. No more trouble."

Luke spit on the ground. "Oh yeah? No more trouble? Are you sure about that?"

Ollie still had his hands up. "What did I do?"

Luke pointed an angry fist at him like he was going to attack.

Luke got into the driver's seat with a slam. He started the Rover and hit the steering wheel in anger. "Goddammit!"

Ollie climbed into the passenger side and shut the door closed. Giving Luke a wise-ass face. He turned to look at me and Steph. "Think she'll be up by the time we get to my sistah's place?" he asked. His lime green shirt glowed ugly as we passed under a street lamp. I groaned inwardly and tried to block out the nightmare I was entering.

Luke started down the side-cut road with a vengeance.

Ollie threw his hand out real fast to scare him. "Made you flinch," he said.

Luke grumbled and breathed fire. "Friggin' seat is too far back," he muttered under his breath. "Goddamnit, can't get it." Was he cooling down? Was my heart regaining its normal pace or starting back up again? Luke got to the intersection and took a left. Toward the winding cliff road. Not in the direction of Ollie's sister's apartment or even the package store. I patted Steph's head as we started climbing up the road. She was still passed out. I was sort of glad she was missing all this. But I didn't feel safe yet.

"Luke, where are we going?" I said, my voice coming out too quiet and cracked. Between the roar of the pavement beneath us and the wind blowing past our ears, he didn't even hear me. Or he was ignoring me. Or he was drunk.

Luke was fumbling with his seat, trying to slide it up to where it usually was.

We turned onto Cliff Drive—the road that led to Mattamuskee Bluff.

"I'm freakin' ten feet away from the steering wheel!" Luke said, giving Ollie a death look. Ollie had adjusted the seat to give himself more leg room when he was driving, and now it was jammed.

The Land Rover was all over the road. I braced myself and swallowed hard.

When Ollie drove us through town, he went faster on the open road, then slow and cautious when making turns. Luke's driving was a little more unpredictable. The road narrowed and became curvy. Sometimes he seemed in control and sometimes he didn't. He anticipated a big curve and slowed way down to get through it. Then he skidded and screeched through another one, landing us clear on the other side of the road. I closed my eyes at one point just to have a little sanity. That didn't help. The barreling of the car as it wove closer to the cliffs turned my stomach.

Luke was speeding, weaving for sure. I could feel it in my racing heart. I could sense it in Ollie's fear. Ollie looked at him and said, "Slow down, man!" He wasn't playing the game anymore. Ollie tugged on the sleeve of Luke's plaid shirt, and Luke shrugged him off. He just pressed the gas harder. Luke knew these turns better. We were getting closer to Mattamuskee Bluff. An image of happy children in the backseat of the Rogers' car flashed in my brain. I touched Steph's shoulder and squeezed. She shook her head and groaned.

"Luke, stop!" I said loudly. He kept his eyes on the road as we sideswiped shrubs and tree branches. "Slow down!" I screamed.

And then I screamed for real.

One. Long. Painful. Cry.

The Land Rover raced up the dark street, spraying

sand under its wheels. I watched the speedometer needle arc to the right. Then it started going back to the left. We started to slow down. A little.

But not nearly enough.

I watched as the speedometer stayed steady, but the entire vehicle began to rush toward the opposite side of the road in slow motion. Luke's hands clenched the steering wheel and tried to veer it right, but we were already heading across the road. Like a slow-moving wave, the Land Rover hit an embankment going the wrong way. Its front wheels bounced off the embankment and sent the vehicle careering back across the road. Luke tried to get us back in control, but it was too late.

The Land Rover headed straight for a boulder at the entrance to the Mattamuskee Bluff parking lot.

Its front bumper connected squarely with the rock, stopping our motion.

Like.

    One.

        Aching.

            Jolt.

I was jerked forward and whipped back into my seat. And that's when I screamed.

Again.

Because the boys went flying.

10 SECONDS AFTER THE ACCIDENT

My hands wouldn't work. I couldn't get my seat belt off. No. The seat belt was broken. It had locked in the crash. No. My brain was not working. It had gotten locked in shock. I yelled for help but Steph was out. I heard moaning from the parking lot.

"I'm coming!" I called.

My seat belt button was jammed. I couldn't get it pushed down. Tears poured down my face, blurring my vision. I heard a cry for help.

"I'm coming!" I screamed. Were words even coming out? Snot ran down my lip and into my mouth. I gagged. I couldn't breathe. Where was I? How could this be real?

"I'm coming!" I said again, although the moaning had stopped.

Click.

The seat belt came free. I let go of the breath I had been holding.

"Steph!" I pushed her, and she grogged something

incoherent. The hood of the car was steaming and sizzling. I should get her out, I should get her out. Away from the smoke. I unbuckled her and she fell to the floor of the Rover. "Steph, get up!" I yelled. She stirred and then pushed herself up to crawling. The side doors were out of shape. I helped her crawl over the side of the car and into the sand. I pulled her arms as she used her knees to crawl away from the car. She wasn't registering anything. We made it to the parking lot and I let go. She lied down on the ground and went back to sleep, resting her head on her elbow as if she were at home.

That's when I saw them. Two dark lumps silhouetted in the glare of the headlights. Two bodies.

One lump was crumpled in front of the few trees that stood in the middle of the parking lot.

The other lump was just beyond the smattering of trees, sprawled out with limbs going in unnatural directions.

I clenched my fists and went toward them.

Where was I? Who was I? Was this really my life?

I got to the trees. They were raggedy trees, beaten down by the sun on this high perch. Three big trees. Thick trunks with some undergrowth. I looked down.

The back of a lime green tennis shirt. I held my hand up to my mouth. There are some things people shouldn't see. Some things to unspeakable to remember. It wasn't the crash into the boulder that killed him. It was the vault through the air. The speed. The force of leaving the vehicle and hitting the tree. The top of Ollie's head was crushed and mangled. His face was smashed in from impact to the tree. He was lying at the foot of the tree with half of his face exposed. It was like shredded beef at the deli. I stood there, frozen, and stared instead at his feet. Tried to avoid seeing the river of blood that was flowing down from his head. I knew in that instant that he was dead.

Then I heard a moan. My name.

"Lucas," I said, his boyhood name coming to my lips without thinking.

I looked past the trees to Luke. He was lying on his back. One knee was going the wrong way and his arm on the other side had a bone sticking out of it. He must have sailed right through this patch of trees, hitting branches as he passed through. I walked carefully around Ollie and went to Luke. It was like my feet were treading through water that rose to my knees. Every step was an effort. I blocked out the headlights with my body for a moment and was able to see Luke's face. His eyes were closed.

"Don't move!" I said. "I'm coming." I knelt down beside him and listened to his chest. His heart was beating. He was breathing.

"Luke!" I cried, too afraid to touch him.

He opened his eyes slowly. Then he said, "I'm not *dead,* April." A little smile lifted in one corner of his mouth.

The horrified look on my face stopped him.

"Ollie is," I said, slow and even like saying it made it real.

"I stood up," Luke said. "And then I fell down again. I think there's something wrong with my leg." I stared at the blood coming from his head, the disgusting bone jutting out of his arm. He was talking as if he didn't even feel the pain.

Then his eyes changed. "What did you say?"

The moon glowed down on me. "Ollie's dead."

Luke craned his neck to look and winced strongly, his head falling back down. He cried out in pain and squeezed his eyes tight. He tried to look again but he fell back in pain. He groaned a loud, guttural cry. Then he lost consciousness.

I looked at Ollie's body quickly before I reached into

Luke's front pocket and pulled out my cell phone. I opened it and turned it on.

We had service.

The 911 operator kept me on the phone as she dispatched the police and ambulances. I knew it would be five or ten minutes since Mattamuskee Bluff was at the highest point of the cliffs. Luke was unconscious, Steph was passed out, so I walked over to Ollie. I knelt down and said, "Ollie? Ollie?" real loud. I thought that maybe I was wrong, maybe Ollie wasn't dead. People survived incredible things. Earlier in the summer, I had read that a toddler survived getting run over by his dad's SUV. Maybe I wasn't actually looking at a dead person. But his head was so mangled. My heart told me to look away. My mind argued.

"What if he is alive?" I screeched into the phone. "What should I do? Should I wrap his head up?"

The woman from 911 paused. Then she said, "Can you get a pulse? Check for breathing?"

His right arm was extended toward me so I took his wrist and put two fingertips to it. I concentrated but didn't feel a pulse. His arm was lifeless. The blood from his head wound was thick and had covered his entire head and was turning his shoulders into a dark, sopping mess.

"You still there? You okay?" the woman's voice on the phone asked.

"Yeah. No. I can't get a pulse!" I said.

"Can you open his mouth and listen for breathing?" Her voice sounded calm and matter-of-fact.

"He's lying on his chest," I said. "His face is gone." I put my ear on his back and listened for the shallowest of movements. I counted in my head. One. Two. Three.

Please breathe. Four. Five. Six. C'mon, Ollie. Seven. Eight. Nine.

"Oh, God, he's gone," I said. My voice broke and I stood up, shaking. I could smell the sweat from his shirt on my face; the blood of his death in my nose.

"Just breathe, honey," she said. "You gonna be okay. They on their way."

"No," I cried—not to her but to Ollie. "No!" I said, shaking my head. This was not supposed to happen. I was not supposed to be here. I was not supposed to see a dead kid. I was not supposed to be at the top of Mattamuskee Bluff, alone in every other sense of the word, not knowing what to do. What to say.

"Just take a step back, honey," she said. "They're turning up Cliff Drive. Two more minutes. How are the other passengers?"

"I don't know!" I cried. "I have to call the Rogers. I have to call Doug."

"Stay with me," the 911 operator ordered. "We will call family in two minutes. You've just gotta stay with me until help arrives."

I started walking away from the accident and toward the cliffs. I took huge hyperventilating breaths.

"Breathe, sweetie, breathe."

I held my breath and listened to the waves crashing below. My feet floated lightly on the rocky dirt. I felt like I was a bird about to take off. "Oh, I'm dizzy," I said into the phone.

"Sit down," the woman said. "Head between your legs."

I ignored her and kept walking toward the edge of the cliff. I focused on the vast black water and the bright half moon. Crescent moon. Whatever the *F* it was.

The occasional crash of waves hitting the rocks sent

me into a trance. I shut the cell phone and put it in my pocket.

Crash. The waves hit the rocks.
Crash. A spray of water tripped up from below.
Crash. The rocks took the impact.
Crash. The wind took away the engine smoke.
Crash. The moon felt no pain.
Then came the sirens.

I ran over to where Steph was so the ambulances wouldn't accidentally run over her in their rush to Mattamuskee Bluff. I tried to pull her up.

"Wake up!" I yelled.

She moaned and her head rolled back and forth. I clapped her cheeks with my hands. "Get up!" I said.

"Oww," she said. But her eyes kept slipping shut.

The sirens grew louder. I put her back down and stood in front of her. First came the headlights, like zigzagging flashlights lost in the woods. As they approached, I waved my arms, but the police cruiser sailed past me and parked beyond the Land Rover. I heard the officer on his radio as the first ambulance arrived right behind him. It parked next to the cop and soon EMTs were rushing out and the cop was heading toward me.

"We're fine," I yelled. "Go to them!" He shined his flashlight at us and doubled back to Ollie and Luke. Two EMTs were around Luke, and two were around Ollie.

"I got a pulse," I heard the EMT next to Luke say. The cop snapped a picture of Luke. Then another picture, farther away, then another. The flash broke up the night sky in pieces.

The other EMT said, "Minor head trauma. Breathing is

stable." They put a brace around Luke's neck and started preparing to load him onto a handheld stretcher.

"Hold his arm," the EMT said to his partner as the cop helped load him onto the stretcher.

Then more police, more ambulances, a fire truck. It was as if the whole force was coming. Cops kept popping out of their cars, looking around, setting up flares, radioing back to headquarters. The two EMTs around Ollie had not sprung into action. They were crouched beside him, but they were not turning him over, were not administering CPR, were not shouting out "Stable" or "Breathing" or "Major trauma to the head." I watched in amazement as Luke was lifted off the ground and an outline of his body in chalk dust was glowing on the dirt. More pictures.

Two new EMTs rushed over to me and Steph. I was just standing there clutching my arms, trembling like I was packed in ice. Steph was at my feet. A female EMT, young, no more than twenty-five, knelt down by Steph and started taking her vitals.

"She drank too much," I said. The woman looked up and then her male EMT partner came over and they put Steph on a stretcher.

"Come with us," she said as they started carrying Steph to the ambulance. I nodded and followed them without a word.

As I walked past the accident, I saw a crowd of cops standing around Ollie. I wouldn't look anymore. I wouldn't watch their faces fall. I stared straight ahead at the back of the ambulance. The door was open. Steph was being loaded in. There was a bench for me to sit on. I climbed up the silver stairs and took my place.

The EMTs left the door open and a cop hopped in and sat down next to me.

"My name's Richard," he said. He was an older guy,

with a grey buzz cut and a bit of a paunch. I read his name tag. It said Col. Morris. "What's your name?"

"April Nichols," I told him, the words coming out hesitantly, as if I were in trouble. The EMTs were hooking Steph up to things and making notes.

Col. Morris looked at me. "And your friend here?"

They were putting an IV in Steph's arm. I told him her name, date of birth.

"How much did she have to drink?"

"I don't know. A lot. We don't usually drink." I shook my head. It felt like I was in some weird TV drama.

The ambulance was so bright. I looked out the back window and it was pitch black, facing the road. I couldn't see the Land Rover or the parking lot. I could barely hear the crashing waves. My brain was starting to mush up.

"How much did you drink?" the officer who had introduced himself as Richard asked me.

He was writing down everything I said. It didn't occur to me not to answer.

"I don't know," I said. "A little."

"One, two?"

I thought back to the keg. I nodded.

"Okay," he said. Then he cocked his head. "We've got a lot to go through. This is just the beginning. I'm going to ask you some questions before this ambulance takes off, and then I'm going to ask you some more at the hospital."

Ollie was dead. Luke was hurt. Steph was unconscious. Richard—Colonel Morris—was acting so cold. Forcing me into the business at hand. How could I answer him when the whole world was falling apart before us?

The EMTs were drawing Steph's blood and taking her temperature. They didn't seem concerned. The female smiled at me but didn't say anything. Was Ollie still lying on the ground? Was Luke being pumped up with morphine?

Richard spoke up. "I repeat. What are the young fellas' names?"

I blinked and looked at him. "Luke Rogers," I said, "the one in the other ambulance."

"The one with the plaid shirt? About 5'8", brown hair?"

I nodded. 5'8"? I guess. I hadn't really thought of his statistics before. I kept answering the questions. I gave him Doug's and Cynthia's name, address, and phone number. I gave the same for Steph's family.

"You're a nanny, you said?" Colonel Morris said, his eyebrow raising.

I nodded.

"And the other fella?"

Ollie. Ollie. Poor Ollie. I whispered his name.

"Did you say O, L, L, I, E?" he spelled out.

I nodded.

"Last name?"

I shrugged and stared at Steph's IV. Clear fluid trickled in.

"You don't know his last name?"

I shook my head. My brain was numb.

"And you jus' said the big guy, he was driving?"

I nodded without thinking.

"And what did you say Luke Rogers' address was again?"

I repeated it, and he said, "Oh, right, same as yours and his parents."

Then my brain went from being numb to being on fire. WAIT—I had answered yes that Ollie was driving. Had I? Colonel Morris had asked it so casually, as if he already knew the answer. *And the big guy, he was driving?* Why did he call him the big guy?

Wait—is that what just happened? Did I just say yes?

Because Ollie had been driving, at one point, but is that what he meant? My head was spinning.

Maybe he didn't write it down.

Maybe he wouldn't ask again.

Maybe Luke would tell him he was driving.

Maybe I had said no.

What did I *say*?

Was Ollie dead? Was he really, really gone? Could it happen that fast? Had I just put my ear on a dead boy's back? What was wrong with me?

"Where were you all going?" Colonel Morris asked. "The cliffs?"

I shook my head. "I don't know."

"You don't know?" he said, studying me. The ambulance's engine started and Colonel Morris got up. He held his finger up to the driver.

"Why don't you know where the car was headed?" he asked.

"Can I call Doug and Cynthia?" I asked.

Richard kept writing and said no. We'd do that at the hospital. Why? Why did we have to wait?

Steph's eyes were fluttering. She looked at me for a second and then closed her eyes again.

"I'm not sure where we were going. Or why."

Colonel Morris started to get impatient. "Okay, okay. We'll finish this at the hospital. We'll start at the beginning. Where you were and what got you to this point."

He closed his notepad and stepped out of the ambulance. I watched as the EMT shut the door and the ambulance pulled out onto the road. As we left the accident, I glimpsed the Land Rover. And then it was gone.

Colonel Morris said we would start at the beginning. The beginning? When Luke arrived at the sliding glass door on the patio? Or when he drove us to Mattamuskee Bluff and we hiked to the peace sign. The beginning when he kissed me on the beach, and we lay together under the stars. The beginning when fell for me . . . when I let myself feel . . . when we lay on the sand, in the safety of the sun, and thought that nothing could harm us except maybe an angry parent.

The beginning when we took four-year-old Hunter to WaterWorld as a prize for lying . . . when we kissed in front of baby Rosy because she was too little to tell . . . when he snuck into my room.

Or my new beginning that started hours ago.

When I saw a different side of him at the party. When I truly feared him in the Rover. When he drove too fast and hit the embankment and skidded across the road until we were jolted by that boulder. The beginning when I didn't even know who he was.

30 MINUTES AFTER THE ACCIDENT

Our accident took over the ER. Luke and Steph were wheeled into separate emergency rooms.

I was put in a private waiting room where Colonel Richard Morris continued to take his report.

I gave him the address of the party, which he radioed in to the station. I imagined the police cruisers racing over there to bust it up, to stop anyone else from making the mistake we did.

I heard Richard's voice in the background. "Miss, miss, please try to focus." His voice came louder and clearer again as my eyes closed to this nightmare. "Now, who did you say was driving again?"

This wasn't the first time he had repeated a question. He'd asked me to repeat lots of details. This one just caught me like a punch to the gut. I opened my eyes wider and looked at his imploring face, the spray of wrinkles around his eyes. He looked tired from years on the force. From crime scenes repeating themselves. From watching young kids die.

"I repeat, who did you say was driving?"

I looked at his badge and said, "Ollie was."

He nodded and wrote it down.

"And where were you headed?"

"I don't know. Ollie took Luke's car and wouldn't give back the keys. I guess we were going to Mattamuskee Bluff. I mean, there's nothing else up there."

Colonel Morris was annoyed that I didn't know the whole story.

So we started at the beginning. Again.

After about ten minutes of telling and retelling the story, Doug and Cynthia came rushing in to my waiting room. Cynthia embraced me in a hug. "Are you all right?" she asked.

I nodded. "My neck is a little sore, but I am okay."

Colonel Morris looked apprehensive when they barged in. He sat back in his seat and took a slow drink of coffee.

Cynthia continued, her face full of dread. "We haven't seen Luke yet. He's in surgery. But I think he's going to be okay."

I squeezed her and tried to reassure Doug with a weak smile. "Yeah, he was unconscious the last time I saw him, at the cliffs, but right after the crash he was talking, so I don't think it's that bad. I–"

Colonel Morris interrupted. "You didn't tell me he was talking."

"Well, I –"

Doug intervened. "I've contacted my lawyer, Diane Williams, who will be representing my family. April can continue her statement at the police station in her presence."

Colonel Morris cleared his throat. He looked at Doug

with an eyebrow raised. "See to it," he said, snapping his notebook shut. Then he saw a nurse pausing before my room in the hallway. "They're ready for you anyway." Richard moved as if he was going to go wait outside the emergency rooms.

Doug said, "Ms. Williams is representing Lucas and Stephanie as well."

Colonel Morris nodded. He smiled at me for the first time. "Thank you for all your patience, April. We'll be speaking together again soon." He looked kind and gentle, a side I had not seen much of before.

I didn't trust it. I needed to get to Luke before he did.

The next few hours at the hospital were a blur. My mind was on shuffle, like an iPod that was broken and would only play bits of things before it switched to the next. Thoughts invaded from everywhere—replaying the night. Thinking back to home and when Steph and I were kids. Reliving the images of Ollie's bloody head. Worrying about Luke in the ER. Tie-dying with Hunter. Lying to the cop. Cleaning off Rosy's spit up from my shirt. Watching Steph make out with Ollie. Greeting Doug and Cynthia when they came home from work.

Wondering what Luke would say when he woke up.

The staff in the ER checked me out and then I was released. Not a cut, not a bruise, no broken bones. Not even official whiplash—just a sore neck from the old 1967 seat belt pulling me back into my seat. No scars on the outside. Just a well of information on the inside fighting to get free.

When I left the emergency room, Doug and Cynthia Rogers were in the general waiting room. Other patients waiting to be seen were right along there with them. Cynthia was tapping her foot on the floor and Doug was staring at the TV screen. When they saw me coming, they both stood up and surrounded me. Cynthia clapped her hands on my shoulders, her short spiky hair and glasses a welcome sign of home. I had been taking care of their children for years, and now they were coming to take care of me.

"Luke's still in surgery," Cynthia said. "I should take you home."

I pictured the beach house and my soft lavender sheets. Hunter downstairs in his Batman pajamas. Rosy in her bare baby chest and diaper.

"Who's with the kids?" I asked.

"Marcy Markson," Cynthia answered. Their neighbor.

"Oh." I thought of Luke's leg all twisted the wrong way. "Umm. I'd like to stay until Luke and Steph wake up."

Doug nodded. "You go, Cyn. Send Marcy back home. I'll call with updates."

Cynthia agreed and hugged him.

"How is Steph?" I asked.

Cynthia looked at me sadly as she grasped her wallet-purse in her hand. "She's stable. They are monitoring her through the night, but it appears that she doesn't have any injuries from the accident." Then she put her arm on my shoulder and her eyes started to get glossy. "I'm so sorry, April," she said. "This is just awful."

She hugged me, and into her shoulder I said, "So you're not mad?"

She shook her head and laughed through her tears. "It wasn't your fault. You two shouldn't have been out with them, but we all make mistakes. You said you girls were going to the movies . . ."

I grimaced and moaned, "We should have. . . ." I

should have never have started lying to the Rogers. I should have never kissed Luke, should have never let him unravel me.

"I shouldn't have lied," I said, "I should have been stronger."

Doug stepped in with a strong hand on my shoulder. "You can be now."

He looked at me intensely and said, "It wasn't your fault." But I could read the question in his stare: *Whose fault was it?*

"I'll be right back," he said as he went to walk Cynthia to her car.

I sat down in a waiting room chair. It was my same body. The feet in sandals I knew so well. The same hands I used every day. But my hands looked like a stranger's. I was exhausted, thinking crazy thoughts, like, I've just won the prize for best summer job story. No one can beat this! Nanny meets manny and falls in love. Then nanny sees dead body and falls apart. Hooray, love and death all in the same summer! Don't worry, she'll be fine by Tuesday for arts and crafts on the patio. The PTSD doesn't set in for a while! I was most definitely going to lose my mind by the end of all this.

The waiting room, although decorated in pastel-patterned fabrics and filled with magazines and a toy section, carried the stuffy antiseptic smell of the hospital. The TV was tuned to the cooking channel. Were they kidding me—that was supposed to be distracting? I watched the man in a white cook's jacket throw vegetables in a wok and lather them with sauces. I wanted to throw up.

Just then a young woman and a man came rushing in through the two sets of automatic doors. He was holding her arm as she half-ran, half-walked to the front desk. She was searching desperately for somewhere to go, someone to see. She was wearing a pajama shirt and jeans and no shoes. Her cell phone was clutched to her ear.

"Yeah, we're here," she said, her voice shaking.

Everyone else in the waiting room stared at the floor, or at the TV, or closed their eyes in rest. No one looked at the woman. Were they averting their eyes to give her privacy because she was trembling, or did they not even notice? I watched as the woman looked around nervously. The nurse at reception came around the desk and met them with a warm, apologetic smile. The woman seemed to collapse momentarily upon hearing the nurse say, "For Mr. Baker?" The man held the woman up and the nurse escorted them down a hallway and out of view. Moments later a guy on a bike came barreling through the ER. He skidded his bike to a halt and dropped it right in front of reception.

"Where is he?" he shouted.

Another nurse escorted him down the same hall.

My heart was like a boulder at the bottom of the ocean.

I waited to see of anyone else rushed in, but no one did.

The static of the waiting room surrounded me.

The chef was adding some risotto.

And then I heard it. An echo of my earlier scream at the accident. But worse. The moaning cry of the woman who had just been escorted down the hall. Into a private waiting room that was not at all soundproof. I heard a thud, like someone punching a wall or knocking a chair over, then another cry of distress. I closed my eyes and let the tears slide down. They had just told them that Ollie was gone.

~ ~ ~

When Doug came back he had a coffee, a bottled water, and two bagels.

"Wanna go eat these outside?" he asked, his tall frame and salt-and-pepper hair a little mussed by the hour.

"Okay," I agreed.

Get the taste of beer out of my mouth. The taste of death.

Doug smiled at me although he was more stressed than I'd ever seen him. For the first time, I noticed how Luke had inherited his father's eyes. When Doug smiled, his eyes crinkled in the same way. Except his eyes were older. And said more.

We walked out side by side, the automatic doors swishing open as we approached and then pausing for a few seconds before shutting closed. We sat on a bench outside the doors and I cracked open the water bottle. I gulped half of it down in one breath. I thought of my beer chugging with Luke and cringed.

"How you holding up?" Doug said, looking at me as he unwrapped a bagel with cream cheese.

I shook my head. "I don't know." Then the tears came again. It was ridiculous. I felt like one of those Mothers Against Drunk Driving ads. This is what you'll turn into if you ride with a drunk driver. Then the camera pans to my blotchy face, red eyes, as I try unsuccessfully to bite into a bagel and instead cover it with tears and snot. "Oh, God."

"April, come here." Doug put his arm around me. "Is this okay?" he asked.

I nodded. It was a fatherly gesture, totally what I needed. I realized in that instant that I had been physically alone since the crash. Except for Cynthia's quick squeeze, my body had been processing this entire thing without being touched. Doug's arm around me as we sat side by side grounded me. It made me feel like I was not alone, that someone was supporting me, that I wouldn't have to let go until I was ready. I buried my face in Doug's shoulder and bawled like an animal. He could have been a stranger I had just met on the street. At that moment, I just needed to let it all go.

"I know," Doug said. "It's going to take a long time."

I blew my nose and got up to throw the tissues away. With my back turned, I blotted my eyes and tried to pull myself together. I sat back down on the bench and it was quiet between us for a minute. No one had emerged from the hospital and the parking lot was still.

Then Doug said, "They didn't give us much information, April. Please tell me what happened."

Colonel Morris's face came to mind.

"What did they tell you?" I asked.

Doug grimaced a little. "Luke's Land Rover hit a large rock along the road just before the parking area at Mattamuskee Bluff. He and Ollie were ejected from the car. Neither of them were wearing seat belts. You know that Ollie . . ."

I nodded.

"You and Steph must have had your seat belts on because you both have no injuries."

"That's right," I said. "We were in the back. I thought they were taking us home, but then he started up the hill, and they were arguing, and –"

Doug looked over his shoulder as he said in a pained way, "Was Luke driving?"

I bit my lip. "No." I couldn't look him in the eye. "Luke had given Ollie the keys hours before, but then Ollie drank too much and decided to take the Rover out."

I started telling the story exactly as it happened at the party. I explained how Steph had also gotten too drunk—and I emphasized that she and I never actually acted like that normally—and how she had gotten into the Rover with him, and then I explained how Luke and I ended up in the vehicle, too, not thinking that he would take off with Luke standing half in and half out.

Doug listened patiently. "You told that cop all of this?"

"Yeah." It was easy to keep my story straight because I told everything as it had actually happened. The only part I skipped over was the swamp road and how they had traded seats. When I described the race up Cliff Drive, I imagined Ollie was still at the wheel. I could replay everything in my head and it almost seemed true. Except when I spoke the words, they sounded false to me. I wondered if Doug could hear the doubt.

He didn't seem to. Colonel Morris hadn't shown any disbelief either.

"Should I have not given Richard the report? Should I have waited? It seemed like the right thing to do, like I *had* to."

Doug sighed and chewed his bagel. "It's a tough call. You're going to have repeat the story several times if they find any discrepancies, say, between your story and Luke's, or evidence at the crime scene."

God, crime scene.

Doug continued, "And debriefing you moments after you witnessed such a traumatic event is . . . questionable. Ethically. You were still in shock. Still are." He was staring up at the moon when he said that last part.

"What do you mean?" I asked. "I was sober enough to remember the whole time at the party, the drive. I was shaken up by the accident, but when he was questioning me in the ambulance and the waiting room, it sort of felt like it was keeping me from falling apart. Like I had an important part to play. That I witnessed it for a reason."

Doug put his arm around me again. "That's very astute of you. April, I know you are trying to help, but you have to be careful not to get caught in the crossfire. You know what I'm saying?" He looked at me meaningfully. "As you go through this procedure, just remember: Don't feel pressured to answer any questions you don't know the answers to. Don't make up an answer because you feel like you *ought* to know. Just say, 'I don't know.' The cops will push and push. That's their job."

Part of me wished I had answered "I don't know" to every single one of Richard's questions. Played the memory-loss card. Played the full-on shock card. Hadn't people actually gone legally blind from experiencing something traumatic? Why couldn't I have just played dumb and not said a single word for one measly hour until I was alone with Doug. Why hadn't I just gone mute with anxiety and then talked the next day once my head was cleared. I looked at Doug and chugged down the rest of my water. I wanted to tell him everything that had happened that summer. Just in those past six weeks. So much had happened I wanted to tell him about. About Luke and me. Little Hunter's accident. Luke's deceit to his parents. My totally distracted brain. I shook my head.

"What if I did something wrong?" I said.

He sat up straighter and looked concerned. "What do you mean?"

I twisted my shoulder and turned to face him. "I mean, what if I said something wrong? To Colonel Morris. What if I was confused or answered something without thinking?"

"April, did you –"

The Accident

Doug was cut off by the sound of the automatic doors opening behind us. He whipped his head around and we saw a nurse coming toward us.

"He's out of surgery," she said. "He's still sedated, but you can see him."

We sprang up off the bench and went rushing inside.

On the way back in, I remembered the people who had come for Ollie. The discarded bicycle was not in front of reception and there was no noise coming from the halls. The nurse led us down to the ER and into Luke's recovery room. He was in a bed, hooked up to all sorts of drips and monitors. The lights in this room were not as bright. He looked both in pain and peaceful. His broken arm and leg were immobilized by straps. The nurse told us that he would be transferred to a room upstairs once he "woke up." She said that if we were staying, she would alert us when he was going to be moved. Doug assured her that we weren't going anywhere. The nurse smiled and gave us directions to a private waiting room that had couches in it where we would be more comfortable.

Doug walked up to Luke's bed and gently touched the side of his face. The side that wasn't covered with a napkin-size bandage. He closed his eyes and took a deep breath in. I watched Luke's slow breathing and said a silent thank you to the moon that had watched over him that night. That had guided his body out of the car and through the grove of trees that could have killed him.

But as Doug and I stepped back into the hall, I wondered why Luke had driven us up to that cliff. Late at night, drunk and angry, what was he thinking? Was he going to hold Ollie over the edge as punishment for taking the Rover? Was he going to scare him by rushing to the cliff and braking at the last second? Should we all be dead?

"Doug," I said, "where did Ollie grow up?"

Doug looked both relieved and sorry to be talking about Luke's friend.

"I knew the Bakers for years. They owned a bunch of property on the edge of town. Got a bundle for it when Target came in and bought the land from them. They moved to California last year. Malibu. Luke met Ollie in high school. You know Luke lived with his mother out in Hingham, so he and Ollie would hook up during summers here. That boy spent a lot of time at our kitchen counter." He shook his head in disbelief.

Doug's quick glimpse into the past reminded me how little I had known Ollie. How I hardly even knew Luke. I didn't even know his friends. His whole life story. His mother's name, for God's sake. And yet I had plunged myself in to falling for him without a care in the world. And now I was answering police questions incorrectly, and then sticking to my false answer. Why?

At the Rogers' house I had a nanny manual on how to keep the kids happy, healthy, and safe.

Where was the manual for this?

SEVEN WEEKS BEFORE THE ACCIDENT

Maybe it was the strong sea air. Maybe it was the immense blue ocean beyond the house. Or maybe it was his to-die-for smile as he stood at the back door, frame pack hanging by a shoulder. One of these things killed my reservation, and I opened the door and let him in.

Mattamuskee Bluff was never the same. Neither was I.

I had just gotten into the first-week groove of my summer nanny job when I heard someone knocking on the pair of glass sliding doors that led out to the back porch. As I walked from the front of the house, where I was cleaning up the kids' lunches in the kitchen, through the living room to where the kids were, I could see him standing there, the ocean a blue backdrop behind him. It was one o'clock on a Monday and we weren't expecting anyone. Especially not on the back porch.

I tilted my head and spoke through the glass door. "Can I help you?"

I knew it was unlocked, but I didn't move to open it.

"Hey, there," he said. His eyebrows raised up like two excited caterpillars and he broke out in a big smile. One of those happy-to-see-you smiles, except I didn't give one back.

"Do I know you?" I said. I glanced over my shoulder at baby Rosy sleeping in her pack-n-play and Hunter having rest time with an episode of Word Wizards.

The guy on the porch was wearing sports sandals, long khaki shorts, a faded blue Varsity T-shirt, and a Red Sox baseball cap. He had a frame pack slung over one shoulder and it looked stuffed to the limit, with a sleeping bag rolled up on the bottom. He put his hand on the outside door handle and started to slide it open as he jokingly mocked, *"Do I know you?!"*

I put my hand on the inside handle and held it closed. A college-age guy, cute, with a trusting smile—weren't people on the news always saying things like the serial killer next door was such a friendly guy?

He laughed. "Umm, have you checked the mailbox out front? It's me. Luke *Rogers*." He slid the door open and lowered his chin like a dog waiting to be pet. Then he saw Hunter on the couch and yelled, "Hey, bud!"

Hunter leaped off the couch and went running to him. "Luke!" he cried, his four-year-old body scrambling to attack him on the porch. Luke's baseball cap got knocked off in the tackle and it all hit me with a wave of sea salt air.

Of course.

I hadn't seen Luke in three years. The last time I saw him he had these weird designs shaved into the side of his hair and he was never without a sports jersey of some kind. By the looks of it, he had grown up some. The last time we saw each other I was a sad excuse for a fifteen-year-old— the only one in my grade still in braces—with a frizzy mess for hair and no chest whatsoever. Well, the chest thing hadn't really changed, but I had grown up, too, and had acquired all these cool survival skills, like confidence, and kicking boys' butts in tennis, and speaking up for myself.

But for some weird reason, Luke's unexpected presence made me revert back to self-conscious mode. "Oh, right"—I stepped out of the way and let him in—"You must think I am totally braindead," I said as I imitated a bobblehead doll. I felt as dizzy as one can of bad-tasting beer made me feel. "He*ll*o, April Nichols."

He left his frame pack on the porch and slid off his sandals before he sat down on the beige living room carpet with Hunter. He immediately started munching on Hunter's sesame seed sticks.

Luke waved away my apologies. "No sweat. I haven't had a true summer in Mattamuskee in years. Not like the old days." He cocked his head at me and winked. He was pretty darn comfortable on that plush carpeting. "It must have been these big buff biceps that confused you." He made a muscle with his arm and laughed. He had been working out, sure, but his arms weren't exactly bulging out of the room. I noticed a tattoo of a snake peeking out from his T-shirt sleeve. "So . . . how are things?" he asked, looking right at me and waiting for an answer.

"Umm, fine," I started. "Yeah, I haven't seen you in years," I said. I had been nannying for the Rogers for the past three summers, ever since Hunter was one. But Luke had gone on to college and always seemed to have a summer job somewhere else. The Rogers were family friends that went back to my mom's med school days. My parents and my younger brother, Ben, and I had spent many summers here in Mattamuskee.

Doug Rogers was Luke's dad from his first marriage, and his wife, Cynthia (my mom's best friend from med school), was Luke's stepmom. Four years ago, Doug and Cynthia had produced Hunter. Now there was Rosy, a squirming, roly-poly baby girl. Great kids, great parents, great house. What could go wrong? I looked at Luke now, all sprawled out on the carpet, watching Word Wizard, and I was glad I had gotten over that crush I'd had on him way back when. The bottom of his feet were dirty and he still had a weird haircut. Minus the sideburn lightning bolts.

"Okay," I said, closing the sliding glass door. "So I think the shock has worn off." I turned to him. "What are you doing here? What's with the backpack?" It came out kind of harsh.

Luke cocked his head toward Hunter, as if to say "Not in front of the kid." Hunter had gotten sucked back into the TV show.

I made a face. "Do you want to talk in the kitchen?" I had my long brownish black hair tied up in a bun on top of my head. I touched it and waited for Luke to respond.

Luke looked at me innocently. "Now?" He seemed to be scanning my bare feet, jean skirt, and white tank top.

"Umm, yeah," I said, rolling my eyes. "Do you know how hard it is to talk over a screaming baby?" We both looked at a placidly sleeping Rosy in her portacrib.

"Gotcha." Luke sprung up and patted Hunter on the head. "I'll be right back, bud."

I followed him as he walked to the kitchen and straddled a counter stool. "So, April, what's up?" he said.

I shook my head. "What's up with *you*? Is this just a friendly visit or what?" I thumbed back to the frame pack on the porch and looked pointedly at his unshaven, stubbly face and grimy hands.

Luke made a joking face. "Yes. I come in peace." He made some kind of alien salute and put on a robot voice. "This. Is. Friendly. Visit."

I ignored the robo-cop impersonation and gave him a semi-serious look. "Then why didn't you come in the front door?"

He was still doing the robot voice. "It. Was. Locked."

At least I had done one thing right.

I cleared my throat. "I'm confused. You weren't in the schedule. You're not on the list. . . ." I looked across the counter to the Rogers' big blue binder. "You know how they are with the nanny manual." Every year I came to sit for the Rogers, the blue binder, their self-made nanny manual bible, always had more pages stuffed into it with instructions on childcare. Anything from AMA articles on child development to kids menus from area restaurants. Playdates and activities were typed onto spreadsheets every week. Daily routines were specific. Time slots ruled. Everything I needed to know about the kids was in the manual. There wasn't one thing in there about Luke coming.

Luke smiled slyly. "Okay, I've got my five-minute pitch, right?"

"Huh?" I said, and started pulling my hair out of its bun. The house and all things domestic and familiar started closing in on me. I had come to think of this beachside home as my own, especially when Doug and Cynthia went to work. Cynthia had rotating hours at the hospital and Doug had long days at the office. This prominent grey-shingled beachhouse was our refuge. I adored it there. The fridge that I filled, the dishwasher that I emptied, the overstuffed beige chairs and couch and all the ocean-colored art on the walls. I was trusted to take care of the kids, and I tried to make everything happy and easy for them. At the end of the day, I could escape to my own room up on the third floor. Rosy's nursery was across the hall, but my room had great views of the ocean and a little deck, too. This summer was more of a challenge because of the baby, but I was ready for it. What I was not ready for, however, was Luke's five-minute pitch.

"Okay, so you know how my dad is like master obsessor about my future and careers and all things real worldly?" Luke was speaking with his hands out like he was ready to catch a football.

"Real worldly?" I said, scrunching my nose. I pulled at the dark brown strands that were freed from my bun.

"Uh-huh." Luke nodded, ignoring my confusion.

"Well," I said, "you mean like following in his footsteps or establishing yourself in some other way?" Doug was a money manager, and an intense kind of guy. He had salt-and-pepper old-guy hair, but it was cut in a young-guy way. He always seemed to be real tan, even in winter.

"Yeah," Luke said. He wrung his hands. "So my dad sort of opened the door to this really good internship at a science lab in Boston –"

"Great," I said, my voice coming out a little uninterested.

Luke held up his hand. "But it totally blew."

"Oh, bummer," I said, still wondering what he was doing here. I thought I heard Rosy making a noise. I held up my finger and promptly turned to go check on her. She was quiet.

"Hunter, need anything?" I asked.

He looked up from the TV and said, "Is Luke still here?"

I nodded and he went back to his snack and show. The Word Wizard was casting a magical spell over a scrambled four-letter word. Hunter was cuddling a couch pillow and looking like he might drift off, too.

When I got back into the kitchen Luke was chugging a neon green power drink.

"So what happened?" I said.

He wiped his mouth on the back of his hand and rolled his eyes. "I just totally couldn't hack it. I showed up late a couple times. I couldn't get the paperwork sorted how they wanted. I didn't even get to the research stage. I mean, honestly, they were pretty anal. They said it wasn't a good match, but I don't know who they expect to fill that position for no pay and no benefits."

"Wow," I said. Cocky much?

Luke continued, giving me his Hollywood smile. "So here's the thing—this is totally, totally okay. Because I realized that it was more *my dad's* dream than mine."

"Oh, okay, he'll probably be glad to hear that tonight." After it came out, I realized how ludicrous that sounded. Doug Rogers was a good businessman, a good father, but when it came to not fulfilling an obligation, there was no way he'd understand that. "Or . . ." I started.

"Or not," Luke finished. "Look, this is beside the point, but I want to go pro—kayaking."

"You want to be a professional kayaker for your job?" I thought he went to BU.

Luke beamed. "Totally. But I have to secure another job or internship before I break the news to him."

"Break the news about the science lab internship or break the news about being a kayaker?" I wrinkled my nose. Where was all this going?

"Both. But the lab one first. That will be easier on all of us."

What did he mean, all of us?

I shook off this insane conversation and clapped my

hands. "Well, good luck then! Should I tell them you stopped by . . . or –"

"Wait!" Luke said. "I've still got my pitch, right?"

I looked at the pile of dirty dishes waiting in the sink. A plate with half-munched celery sticks and peanut butter stood on the counter. "Oh, right."

"Look, I know you have your hands full here. And I am *so* not trying to complicate things. But I just need to clear my head for a couple days. Get my shit together. Apply for a few jobs, get things organized, and then once I do, I'll give full disclosure to my dad and Cynthia."

"Oh . . . kay," I said, "so you *don't* want me to tell them you stopped by. You want me to pretend this never happened until you come and tell them yourself."

Luke's mouth popped open. His tongue was neon green. "Yes!" he said. Then he gripped my shoulders in what was supposed to be a kind gesture of thanks. I was annoyed at myself for noticing how tan those arms of his were. His haircut wasn't actually that weird. It was sort of a mix between a preppy haircut grown out or a skater cut trying to look decent.

I stepped back and shook his hands off of me. "So then why did you come by at all?"

He kept grinning. "So I can stay in the basement, of course!" He came forward again for one quick maniacal squeeze of my shoulders and then headed for the porch. I watched him as he picked up his frame pack and motioned to go down the outdoor cellar stairs.

I stood there staring at the sliding glass door, which he had left open, and the vast blue ocean beyond. The wind was whipping the tall tigerlily grasses in the backyard, and I knew in that instant that I should follow him and tell him that this wasn't going to work. But for some reason, as the Word Wizard sounded out the word "book" for Hunter, I didn't. I just closed the sliding glass door. Then I turned the lock.

I sat on the couch reading books to Hunter for half an hour, wondering what Luke was doing down in the basement. It was partially refinished and had a half bath. But the idea that he would rather sleep on the cold floor than face his father worried me.

These were my employers.

What if I made some horrible mistake on the job? How would Doug and Cynthia react? Rosy was only four months old. She was more of a wild card. Babies got dropped and choked on things and couldn't even talk to tell you where it hurt.

As if on cue, when I finished the last book in the stack, there he was again, staring in at us from the sliding glass door. Hunter sprang up and I followed him to unlock the door. Luke entered and I gave him a disapproving look. "This is really not part of the schedule," I said.

He patted my shoulders. "I know," he said, all sorts of sincerity dripping along with the sweat on the ridge of his forehead. Was he doing push-ups down there? "And you are so much more responsible than I am. Don't think I don't fully appreciate that."

I started to say, "But you're asking me to *lie* –" but he cut me off.

"Just hear me out," he said, "this is totally short-term." Luke kneeled down and looked at Hunter. "Bud, I need your help."

Hunter's eyes grew wide and it was obvious that he adored his older stepbrother.

Luke walked Hunter over to the big white board in the

kitchen. He circled Thursday with a red marker, three days from now. "Can you keep my being here a surprise until this day?"

Hunter opened his eyes wide and said, "Why?"

Luke ruffled his light brown crew cut like he was inducting Hunter into the magical world of adulthood.

"Because," he said, looking serious, "I am waiting until that day to give Mom and Dad a big surprise. But if they know I am here before then it will ruin the surprise."

Oh my God, he was waltzing right in and making the poor kid lie to his own parents.

Hunter was elated. "What's the supwise?! What's the supwise?!" he squealed.

Luke whispered something in his ear. What, was he promising him roller coasters, ice cream cake every night before bed, endless video games??

Hunter started jumping up and down and bounced into the other room, grabbing a life-size stuffed dog and wrestling it under the dining room table.

"Luke, this isn't–" I started. "I really don't think you should be–"

Luke looked at me, hopeful. "You've messed up before, right?" he said. "You know where I'm at?"

I shook my head. No, I actually hadn't really messed up in that major of a way.

"Why here?" I said. "What about your mom's?"

He bit his lip. "Worse."

"But you're . . ."—I calculated his age in my head—"twenty, right?"

He sighed out. "Exactly."

Too old to be doing this or too old to be parented by his parents?

"I just need two days," he said like an honest-to-god salesman.

I looked at the dry-erase board. "Three."

"Four max," he said, giving me a sexy smile.

I shook my head. This went against everything I'd ever been taught. I imagined my parents back home in western Massachusetts shaking their heads at my judgment. "And you lied for him, April?" I could hear my mom saying. "You're smarter than that, sweetie," my dad's imaginary voice rang out.

Hunter came tripping back in, the toy dog in a headlock.

I had pulled all of my dark brown hair out of its bun and was combing my fingers through it. "So what's in it for me, Luke?" I asked, giving him my unspoken okay.

"Yes!" he said, pumping his elbow backward. He did a little athletic hop. "You won't be sorry, April," he said. "I swear to you, I owe you big time." Luke put his hands up like he was raising the roof.

I held on to the edges of my short jean skirt and gave him a skeptical look.

He ignored it.

Hunter started, "We're gonna get–!"

Luke clapped his hands over Hunter's mouth and said, "Remember, bud, not until the circled day, okay?" Then he smiled at me. "I gotta check my e-mail. Is the laptop turned on?"

Hunter went dashing toward the computer room like a dog off his leash, and I picked up the nanny manual.

We were totally off-schedule, and there was nothing in the nanny manual about making mistakes.

Luke disappeared twenty minutes before Doug and Cynthia's train got in from Providence. They pulled into the detached garage simultaneously, each driving a matching silver Volvo—sedan and station wagon versions—and I watched the electric doors opening and closing in sync. Then they emerged from the garage's side door and walked up the little manicured path to the front door. Cynthia had tiled a mosaic walking path and they had planted a bunch of bonsai-type of shrubs. Cynthia was a little OCD on keeping everything in proper order, how the shoes should be lined up in the mud room, which order the milks should run in the fridge (soy milk on the right, cow milk in the middle, and her pumped breastmilk on the far left). She entered the house with a smile as she nodded her spiky brown head of hair at us. Hunter was drawing at the kitchen counter and Rosy was strapped to my chest as I prepped dinner.

"Mommy!" he exclaimed, not rising from the counter.

"Hi, sweets!" She blew him a kiss as she headed upstairs. She didn't give hugs and kisses until she was out of her scrubs and showered. Doug, on the other hand, barged in with a bellow and Hunter went scrambling toward him. Rosy kicked her feet a little as she waited for attention.

It was good timing because the stove was just heating up with rice, stir fry, and chicken in one pan and tofu in another. I needed to add spices and sauces and set the table and it was always safer when I could put Rosy down. All my mom's cooking lessons over the years had served me well.

Doug extended his arms for her and I passed her off. As he settled into the living room with the kids, I thought of Luke down in the basement. Was he directly beneath his dad right at that moment? Or was he lying on his sleeping bag on the basement floor under me, in the kitchen, listening to his iPod? Maybe he was in town getting pizza. I looked out the window and wondered when I'd see him again.

~ ~ ~

That night at dinner, Hunter was wiggling in his seat like it was alive.

"How was your day, sweets?" Cynthia asked.

Hunter's wiggling increased as his wooden junior chair seemed to transform into a pony.

"Gooood!" he exclaimed, covering his mouth and giving me an obvious, guilty smile. He still had a ring of brown around his mouth from a pre-dinner macaroon snack. Oh God, here it came. Four-year-olds could not be trusted.

Cynthia's eyebrows raised and she turned to me. "Monday is music class, no?" she said, tilting her head back to the white board and checking the kids' activities schedule.

I nodded and took a big bite of sautéed chicken and rice. Yep, we sang and danced and played with instruments from 10:30-11:15, as expected. But music class wasn't giving Hunter the wiggles.

He pointed up at the calendar and stifled an explosion of laughter. The big red circled Thursday loomed above. Four-Year-Old's First Lie.

"Oh good, you remembered to circle my speech day on the calendar," Cynthia said, noticing it.

"Hhmm?" I said, choking down a string bean.

"You are so on top of things, April," she said, pulling the nanny manual onto her lap like it was a reference guide she used on the OBGYN floor to choose medications for patients. "Look, Doug, she's reading ahead." She pushed the manual over and I saw that on Wednesday's agenda it asked me to remind her about a speech she was giving at a hospital in Boston the next day.

I smiled and wiped my mouth on a cloth napkin. "It's funny you should say that, because —"

Hunter let out a loud burp and laughed.

Doug gave him a disapproving look. "What do you say?"

"Excuse me," Hunter squeaked out. He was trying to be quiet, but I could see that he was about to lose it.

"Umm, yeah," I said, glancing at the sliding glass door and picturing Luke standing behind it. "So something really strange happened today..."

Hunter dropped his fork and it went clanging to the hardwood floor below. Rosy started to cry and Cynthia picked her up and started walking her around. Doug wasn't even listening to me. He was just silently pointing at the fork and giving Hunter eye signals to pick it up.

"Yeah, I just thought maybe we should talk about..." I tried again.

Rosy was fussing, and since I was technically off-duty now, Cynthia had abandoned her half-eaten plate and was patting Rosy's back and walking toward the stairs. Cynthia turned to me before she was out of view.

"I'm sure you did fine. Can you write me a note?" she mouthed, and pointed her head toward the smaller dry erase board that was for any questions that came up during the day.

I nodded and started to say, "Well, it was about that red circle there," when Hunter came up from behind and clasped his hand over my mouth. His hot breath fogged over my ear as he tried desperately to whisper without being heard by anyone but me. "Da supwise!" I heard him say, and *"Sshh!"*

I realized then and there that any trusted adult could make a child lie and believe it was just a fun game. And for me, in that moment so many weeks ago, lying for Luke wasn't *that* big of a deal. I nodded to Cynthia as she walked away with Rosy, and I agreed to write a note on the dry-erase board instead of telling her Luke had lost his internship and was hiding out in the basement. It wasn't my problem, I rationalized. It wasn't even *about* me. After all, like Luke said, it would only be for a couple days.

THE MORNING AFTER THE ACCIDENT

I awoke to the sound of a strange woman's voice saying, "Honey, who are you waiting for? Honey, wake up." I opened my eyes to see a nurse in pale peach scrubs leaning over Doug and tapping him on his wrist. I peeled my face from the vinyl couch as Doug sat up in a haze. His salt-and-pepper hair was sticking up on one side and he was reaching for his glasses. There were no windows in the waiting room, so I didn't know how long we had fallen asleep, but my body felt like it had been squooshed into the pleather couch for a long time.

"Luke Rogers," Doug said, straightening his shirt. "We are waiting to be told when he is released from ER and moved upstairs."

The nurse looked at him like he was crazy. "Honey, I been on shift for three hours and there ain't no one named Lou Rogers in the ER."

Doug stood up.

"It's *Lukas* Rogers. And you've been on duty for three

hours and this is the first time you've noticed that we're here?"

The nurse arched her back and swiveled her neck around. "Excuse me, sir, this is the ER—major trauma and *emergencies*. Forgive me if I have been taking care of patients while you slept." She began to strut out the door without looking back.

We got up and headed out of the ER wing, toward the main hospital. We followed signs for the information desk. I felt naked without my bag or Hunter's hand to hold or Rosy on my hip. But the kids had no knowledge of what we were going through, and my bag had been left behind after the accident. Even though the Land Rover had probably been towed away by then, I still pictured it steaming and sizzling on that cliff, even as the sun rose. I imagined that Ollie was not bloodied and crumpled by the tree. But that he rolled over and dusted himself off.

He said, "Hey, guys, look, good as new. It was just a joke. I got you good, huh?"

After several minutes of walking, we saw the information desk. It was set back in a corner and surrounded by glass walls. When we went to open the glass door, it was locked. Doug knocked on the glass to get the young guy's attention behind the desk. The guy pointed over to a phone on a nearby desk. Mechanically, we turned to read a sign over it that said, "Press 1 for information." Doug picked up the receiver and punched 1 into the phone. As it rang, I watched the guy in the glass box pick up his phone.

"Good morning, this is Information. How may I help you?"

Doug turned to look at the guy. He shook his head and asked for Luke's room number and floor. The guy put us on hold as he went to retrieve the information. I saw him take another call while we waited. What kind of a hospital was this? When he returned, he directed us to Luke's room in a very chipper tone. Doug grunted "Thanks" and slammed down the phone. We headed to the elevators.

When we got to Room 33, the door was closed, so we doubled back to the nurse's station to confirm. We didn't want to bust in on a different patient. The nurse, a pale woman with thin white-blond hair that bobbed around her jaw, slowly thumbed through her book as we waited.

"Yes, that's right. Thirty-three. I just need you to sign here in the visitor's section." She thumbed to another part. "Oh, wait. He already has a visitor. You might want to wait. It's a Colonel Richard Mor –"

Doug slammed his hands down on the counter and started booking to Luke's room. I heard the nurse saying, "Sir? Sir?" as we rushed away, but she did not get up off her seat. When we reached the room, Doug composed himself and gave a swift knock before entering.

Luke was under some thin white blankets, all bandaged up with IVs attached.

Colonel Morris was sitting on a chair by the window.

"Dad," Luke said as we entered. "April. Thank. . ."

We went to opposite sides of his bed. I touched his hand on his good arm and Doug patted the top of his good foot. Luke looked at me as though I were an angel.

"Dad, what happened? This guy won't tell me anything." He thumbed over to Colonel Morris.

Richard stood up. "That's what I've been trying to gather from *you* for the last two hours. What you remember."

Luke spoke defensively. "I told you! I don't remember anything."

Doug held up his hand. "Colonel, I appreciate your vigilance in this case, but per his lawyer's request, my son will withhold any further statements until he is released from the hospital."

Luke's eyebrows went up.

He suddenly realized the gravity of the situation.

"Understood," Richard said. "I will leave you to your family. Thanks for your cooperation, Luke." He nodded as he left the room.

Doug stood up and shut the door behind him.

When he came back, Luke was speaking quietly. "What happened? What's going on?"

Doug held out his hands for Luke to stop. "Just slow down. Please bear with me for a moment. That cop shouldn't have been in here talking to you. God. No wonder they have to have ankle and bracelet alarms on the new babies. Any bozo could come in here at any time of the day."

"Dad! What happened?"

Luke's eyes were worried and searching the distance in his father's demeanor. Doug turned to him. "Luke, tell me the last thing you remember."

"Nothing! I blacked it all out. I don't remember anything!"

"Do you remember having dinner with us?"

Luke was steaming now. "Well, God, of course. Yes. Dinner was before the party. We had salmon and peas. What I don't remember is what landed me here. Did I get shot? In a fight? Run over? What?"

Doug was calm and persistent. Luke was pleading me with his eyes to tell him what was going on. *I want to, Luke,* I thought. *I want to tell you everything.*

"Luke," Doug said, "what was the last thing you remember at the party?"

Luke closed his eyes and looked at his blanket. "I don't know. Standing at the keg with Mike. Talking about dog races or that new punk band out of Prov. Some such shit. I don't know. Getting hammered."

Forcing your girlfriend to chug a beer? Yelling "I love you" megaphone-style for the whole neighborhood to hear? Trying to rescue your Rover? He didn't remember those things?

"That's the last thing?" I said.

Doug gave me a look that said "Stay out of it."

"Getting hammered, that's what you remember?" Doug said, anger rising in his voice. "You're lucky the hospital won't release your toxicology reports to the police."

"God, Dad, you're worse than the cop," Luke said. "Yeah, the keg in the kitchen is the last thing I remember. I blacked out the rest. What do you want me to say?"

Doug spoke slow and even. "Your Land Rover crashed up at Mattamuskee Bluff. Ollie and Steph were also in the car. So was April." He looked at me apologetically. "Steph's okay."

Luke waited for more.

Doug finished. "Son, Ollie didn't make it." He closed his eyes.

Luke's face morphed into one of disbelief. "What?"

Doug nodded and went to his son. He started to say, "I'm so sorry" but got choked up, his anger melding into disbelief.

Luke whispered, "Ollie?" He choked up and tears started to form. "And I was *driving*?" He said it as if he couldn't actually believe he had been.

Doug shook his head, rubbing Luke's neck. "No. Ollie was."

Luke looked at me, searching my eyes for understanding.

He said, "Ollie was driving the Rover?"

I touched his hand and looked at his scared eyes and fragile body.

I nodded. "Yeah, he was."

Double gulp.

Luke gave me a look that bore right through me. "Oh," he said as relief poured out of him. He looked at me meaningfully. "I guess that should make me feel better, but right now, it just doesn't. Why was he driving?" Then he grimaced at his father. "He's dead?" he said in disbelief.

I shrugged and tried to answer Luke's question. "I don't know. You gave him the keys earlier in the night. He was drunk. There wasn't a lot of rational thinking going on."

Doug stepped away and stood at the window with his back to Luke. Luke held my hand and stared out the window, too. He squeezed the pump on the IV so more pain medicine would flow out. I waited with him for a while as the three of us held to our own thoughts. Mine were wavering between running and screaming or finding a nice quiet place to curl up in.

"I have to go find Steph," I said. "But I'll come back."

Doug nodded and turned back to the window. As I walked backward out of the room, Luke mouthed "I love you" to me. I smiled and mouthed "I love you, too." But part of it just felt like something you say.

Steph was taking a shower when I found her room in the hospital. I called into the bathroom that I was there and she said she would be right out.

A few minutes later she came out, red-faced from the shower, her hair wound up in a towel, and wearing a strange button-up shirt. It looked like something an old lady had died in as she was reliving the best year of her life, 1967.

"What is that?" I said, pointing to the polyester shirt. I needed to pretend this wasn't happening.

She pulled on the butterfly collar. "The hospital's stash of extra clothes. It was this or my pukey shirt from last night." She sat down on the bed next to me, real slow like she was hurtin'.

I gave her a hug. She tilted her head and looked at me sadly. "I really messed up, huh?" She rubbed her eyes and said, "God. I feel like crud."

I put a strand of hair behind my ear. "We all really messed up. Are you hungover?"

She nodded. "Uh-huh. Severely. Ibuprofen helps. And the banana I ate. *It could be worse.*"

We shared a look that said the unspoken: Ollie.

"What do you remember?" I asked.

"I remember bits and pieces of everything. I remember you getting me out of the car. The cold dirt parking lot on my face." She looked at me hard. "It's so crazy."

"Ollie's *gone*," I whispered. I hardly knew him, but I could hardly believe it.

She shook her head. "I know. It's, like, insane." Steph started chewing on the end of her towel.

Then I started to panic. I wasn't used to lying, but I had always heard that if you tell one lie, it leads to another, and another, until you have a whole spiderweb of lies going on. I realized that my lie to Colonel Morris had already started spider webbing. First I lied, then once I realized it, I lied again. What was I thinking? Then I expanded that lie and told him the story with Ollie driving the whole time. Then I lied to Doug about it even though he could have helped me understand why I was lying and how to retract it and protect myself. Here I was with Steph, the one person in the world who I told everything to, who knew me better than anyone. Could I tell her what I had done?

"This whole process has been crazy," I started. "The police interrogation. The hospital staff."

Steph looked concerned. "How's Luke?"

"Huh?" I blinked. "Oh, uh. We just told him about Ollie. It was pretty intense."

"So Doug and Cynthia know about you two?"

"No!" I pulled on the sheet on her bed. "No one does! You can't tell anyone!"

Steph looked at me strangely, the towel wedged in the corner of her mouth. "Why do I still have to keep this a secret?"

"It's complicated!"

Steph squinted. "Oh-kay. . ."

"Steph, about Luke, he has no memory of what happened. Zilch. Zero. Nada."

"So?"

"So *I do*. I remember everything. What about you. Do you?"

"Have memory of the accident? No." She shook her head and the towel came loose. "I remember *after* the accident, a little. I think I saw them on the ground in the shine of the headlights." She winced at the memory or her headache.

I grabbed her wrist. "Doug doesn't want any of us talking to the police without a lawyer being present."

Steph narrowed her eyes. "Are you okay? What's going on?"

I squeezed her wrist so she would listen for half a second. "Steph! Cops cans screw you. All of us. And Luke wasn't driving, Okay? He wasn't behind the wheel when it crashed. Ollie was driving. He killed himself and he almost killed Luke. If I hadn't fastened your seat belt around your passed-out body, you'd be dead, too. Okay?" At least that was probably true.

Steph pulled her wrist back from my grip. "You're freaking out. You're freaking *me* out. Why are we freaking out?" She took the towel off her lap and threw it on the floor. Her wet curls bounced around her head as her head shook.

"Listen. Luke is in some serious trouble if the cops don't believe me."

Steph was wide-eyed. "Why wouldn't they believe you?"

Of course, she had never known me to lie. Not to her, not to anyone. And why would I lie about something so serious?

"Steph, I am just saying. Giving a statement is a huge deal. Don't put yourself through that. Especially if your memory is spotty. *And* an intoxicated memory. It can get really messy."

She pulled her hair back into a ponytail and stared at me. "I'm confused," she said, but she wasn't talking about the accident. She was talking about me. Steph got up from the bed and picked up the towel. She brought it to the bathroom and put it in the soiled-towels hamper. She came back in and looked at me as if she were waiting for an explanation. I looked at her with remorse and shrugged a little. I couldn't spill the whole story out to her right there in the hospital room.

Two reasons.

One: I didn't actually trust that she wouldn't go to the police with the confessed information.

And two: Cynthia was at the door, ready to take us home.

The Accident

~ ~ ~

I didn't expect my parents to be at the Rogers' house when Steph and I came home from the hospital. I felt like a baby running into my mother's arms, wiping away my tears on my dad's T-shirt. I was supposed to be in Mattamuskee proving myself, not falling to pieces when I saw my parents. I wanted to tell them everything. I wanted them to fix it for me, tell me what I should do.

I had children to nanny for. Hunter and Rosy. How was I going to do this? I had to tell them. But when we went for a walk along Crescent Beach, I kept it all in.

My parents offered me everything. To take me home. To send me back to the hills of western Mass and take over my job for me. Care for Hunter and Rosy. Stay at the beach house with me during my last week of nannying. Or to have Steph stay on and help me nanny. They had endless ideas.

"I'm fine," I told them, getting angry for no apparent reason. "I can do this. I didn't break my leg or anything."

"You witnessed a terrible thing," my father said. The experience of his own years called to me, but I wouldn't listen.

"You don't have to finish this job. We can work something out," my mom said. She was practical and addressing my immediate state. "Let us help you."

"I don't want you to stay," I said. "I want you to go."

I couldn't leave now. I had to stay and figure things out.

SIX WEEKS BEFORE THE ACCIDENT

Luke had been hiding out in the basement like some new-age squatter, and Cynthia and Doug were none the wiser. They did breakfast and dinner with the kids routinely, while I bit my nails, expecting Luke to get caught sneaking in or out. And then expecting *myself* to get caught for concealing a fugitive. But he didn't. And I didn't.

I really couldn't stand keeping it a secret. But life came first. Kid life, that is. I buckled Rosy into the jogging stroller, fastened Hunter's bike helmet, and we were off and running to Hunter's *Español on Tuesdays!* class at the library.

I had left a small note for Cynthia on the dry erase board that said "Can we chat about a visitor??" I thought that might be a good way to ease into telling her that Luke was here. I totally couldn't hold it in anymore. It just wasn't right. She had written back "Yes!" but had left for work before we could Discuss with a capital D.

I checked Yahoo weather on the way to Spanish class and saw it was showing four days of sun icons in a row. I reassured myself that it was a good sign. That the wholesomeness of their town was the ultimate good sign. Bad things didn't happen here.

The town of Mattamuskee, Rhode Island, was right on the ocean and it was sweet and safe and beautiful. The Rogers' house overlooked Crescent Beach, and it was just a quick ten-minute walk down to the shore. Crescent Beach was a great kid beach because the waves weren't too rough, there were boats to look at, and there were tons of snails and shells to find in the muddy sand.

Hunter pedaled ahead of us on his little bike with training wheels and I shouted out signals like "Stop ahead!" or "Turn right!" He didn't have his lefts and rights down, but he knew where we were going. I loved the sense of *knowing what to do* that I had with him. I loved teaching him left from right. I loved being in charge and knowing I was keeping him safe. I gazed down at the empty beach and its pale glow of morning sun. I felt a special connection to the ocean even though I didn't grow up right next to it. Maybe it was from all the times we visited.

My parents and my fourteen-year-old brother Ben and I had been coming to Mattamuskee for years before Hunter and Rosy were born, even before Cynthia had met Doug. My mom and Cynthia went to med school in Boston way back when, and actually Ben and I had lived in South Boston when we were little. When I started Kindergarten, my parents had moved us two and a half hours west of Boston, to a little podunk town out in the hills of western Massachusetts.

It worked out well because my dad had reinvented himself from an employee in the Boston Highway Department to a hippie-kind of arborist out in the country. He cut down trees and did landscaping and that sort of thing. For a guy who was originally from the working class neighborhood of Southie, this was a huge change for him. He never let us forget how lucky we were.

My mom was also from Southie, and the only way out she saw was to become a doctor or a lawyer. She got scholarships and worked her butt off to be the first college graduate in her family. *She* never let us forget *this*. She and Dad struggled through it all and made a better life for us. I thought of our little house in the middle of the woods. We had a really great view of this one particular hill and in the summer at night the whole place just came alive with the sounds of crickets and then, in the morning, we awoke to the sound of birds. I thought of my parents and my brother Ben at home and how this was now my last summer before college.

Little did I know then, though, when Hunter and I were making our way into town for Spanish class, that Mattamuskee would be the place where I would have to prove myself.

We made our way down its narrow, brick sidewalks and into the quaint downtown. The former one-room schoolhouse had been transformed into an upscale seafood restaurant. The firehouse still stood in its original brick building with grand arches, but across the street was a new wireless-access coffeehouse. We walked past a couple boutiques, the old-fashioned drugstore, and headed for the library made of rounded stone with a cupola on top. A man jogged by with a golden retriever. An older mom pushed her blond-haired twins up to the library's handicapped-access entrance. It was a nice, family-oriented town. No need to panic.

But panic was on the menu.

I felt excited energy rise in me as we walked inside the library and I saw him. Sitting at the public computer, printing out a letter and addressing an envelope.

"Luke?" I said, coming up behind him, my voice coming out all school-teacher-y.

He turned around in the swivel chair and checked his watch. "Class starts in two minutes," he said. "I'll still be here when you're done."

I furrowed my brows at him for his lack of explaining why he was there and adjusted Rosy on my hip. His heels were pushed up out of his sports sandals, revealing muscular calves, as he worked at the desk, and he looked freshly showered.

"Umm, oh . . . kay," I said as Hunter pulled me toward the braided rug where we would start pronouncing *"Hola!"* and *"Como estás?"* with hand puppets.

I gave Luke a questioning look as we walked away, and I swear out the corner of my eye I could see him smiling.

As expected, Luke was still at the library after our Spanish session with Señora Harrison. He was sitting with legs spread in a lounge-y leather chair reading the *New York Times* when Hunter went pile-driving toward him.

"Library," I reminded him as we all exited, "*sshh.*"

Luke opened up the straps on Rosy's stroller and helped me put her in. Before I could say thanks he was pushing the stroller forward with one hand while giving Hunter a little nudge to get him started on his bike.

Damn, boy.

We started walking and I felt naked without a stroller to push or a baby carrier strapped on my body. My bag was in the bottom of the stroller so my arms were just these hanging appendages.

"Do you want me to push it?" I said, reaching for the stroller.

Luke shook his head easily. "I don't mind pushing it." Then he added, "Actually, I kind of like it."

I peeked over at him. Okay. . . . I jogged up the sidewalk so I could be ahead of Hunter, using my arms to direct him left and right. I looked back a couple times to see Luke Bogarting my job and smiled at him with mini cheerleader waves. I was *so* not a cheerleader. Why did I feel annoyingly nervous around him?

Rosy spit her pacifier out a couple times and Luke bent down to get it. At one point I saw him shove it in his mouth to clean it off and then give it back to her. That was kind of gross, and I wasn't sure how hygienic that was, but I guess it was better than using one of those toxic baby wipes. Luke trotted up alongside us and I noticed that not only were his arms really tan and nicely shaped, but he actually had an overall strong body. Wow. He had really changed in three years. Hot *and* responsible? Well, maybe responsible was stretching it. He was hiding out in the basement after all.

I wondered what he thought when he looked at me. I wasn't the babe in the room that guys automatically gravitated toward, but I wasn't a troll either. I guess my nicest physical feature was my light bluish-grey eyes set against my very dark brown hair. One time this guy I used to be in love with, Matt Lapinski, said my eyes had the color of the ocean inside, and sometimes they looked like a clear winter-blue sky, but I always wondered if he focused on my eyes because the rest of my body was just more or less *blah*.

It didn't really matter because Luke was smiling like it was his job. I wasn't sure if this was how he was all the time or if this was flirting. My flirting radar was kind of rusty. Matt Lapinski was, like, eight months ago and there hadn't been much action since. Not counting that skater kid Noah

The Accident

I met at prom.

When we reached the house, Luke pulled his bike messenger bag over to his front and addressed Hunter. "Hey, bud, you want a banana?" Hunter ditched his bike in the middle of the driveway and scrambled up to Luke.

Luke unzipped his bag and pulled something invisible out of it. He held an imaginary banana in one hand and peeled it with the other. Hunter was holding the fly of his shorts as his legs did a wiggle dance.

"Mmm, yummy," Luke said, taking a bite in the air and then handing it over to Hunter.

I stole a glance at Luke as I unbuckled Rosy and lifted her out of the stroller. Hunter was chomping away at his invisible banana when Luke caught my eye.

"You want one?" he asked, looking down into his bag.

"Okay," I said, nodding and feeling a little embarrassed. "Sure." This guy had definitely spent some time with kids. He was a lot different than the boys at home. As I nibbled the invisible banana in the driveway, I wondered if Luke could see right through me. I knew he was watching me so I played the game and pretended to give Rosy a bite.

"She can't eat real food yet!" Hunter squealed, "just baby bottles!" He collapsed to the gravel driveway in a canned fit of laughter. Then he said, "I have to go potty!"

I looked up and saw that Luke was still watching me.

"What?" I said.

"After you finish your banana," he said, "do you want to go up to Mattamuskee Bluff?"

~ ~ ~

"I have to go to the grocery store before lunch, and then *make* lunch, before Hunter's rest time," I said as Luke loaded the car seats into his 1967 Land Rover. The nanny manual would have had us building with blocks and then painting with watercolors at this time, but I figured we could squeeze one of the activities in before Hunter's 2:30 swim lesson. Watercolors, for sure. Because of the evidence left behind that we had actually done it: a bright shining sunshine-and-rainbow painting confirming that I hadn't slacked on my duties.

I got in the front seat and buckled up. Luke buckled his seat and lowered his sunglasses onto the bridge of his nose. "You ready?" he said, 1980s Tom Cruise-style.

"You are such a nerd," I said, rolling my eyes.

He opened his mouth wide as he backed out the driveway. "Ah! A nerd? These sunglasses cost forty-five dollars!"

"Ballsy," I said.

"Yeah, I know. Do you know how often I lose sunglasses?"

We pulled onto the street and started heading back through town and out to the side roads. "No," I said, "I meant about parking your car two streets over."

"Not as ballsy as you'd think," he said. "Dad and Cynthia are like automatons. They never turn right out of the driveway. Not during the week. It wouldn't make sense for getting to the train station."

"Well, okay," I said, "and seeing as this situation is only *temporary* maybe you don't care if you get caught..."

"Caught shmaught."

I cleared my throat. "Your stepmom is a *doctor*. She has a rotating schedule with different hours every few days. And I've been told she sometimes likes to go up to Mattamuskee Bluff to meditate."

"Meditate, my ass!"

"Luke!" I said. I wanted to add *Watch your language,* but

instead I turned to see if Hunter had overheard. He seemed to be paying close attention but not saying anything.

"What?" Luke smiled. A smile to die for.

Luke didn't seem too concerned about scoring the next job. And my job? Well, it wasn't exactly going according to plan. But I was going to get it back on track that night when Doug and Cynthia came home. I pictured the dry erase board with my note about a visitor.

Visitor, *my* ass! I thought.

Luke cruised through the town, crossing under yellow lights with seconds to spare.

"I can see why you chose the basement over your car," I said, looking at the old-fashioned Land Rover. "Is this no-windshield thing even legal?" I added.

Luke grimaced. "Kind of. It's sort of *stuck* this way." The wind was whipping through our hair more strongly now that we had turned onto a larger road that led to Cliff Drive. "Does all the wind bother you?"

I shook my head. It actually felt really cool. In both meanings of the word.

As we passed a little duck pond, Luke turned up Cliff Drive and we began the ascent to Mattamuskee Bluff. Hunter was letting cheese puffs escape his fingers and float over his head on the wind. Rosy, whose car seat was facing backward, had probably fallen asleep since she was quiet.

"So are you headed off to Harvard or something?" Luke asked. He said it in a nice way.

"Why do you say that?" I was actually going to a school near Boston, but it wasn't Harvard.

"Miss Straight-A's," he said, slowing down to navigate the narrow road.

"I didn't get straight-A's," I said. I hadn't been up to Mattamuskee Bluff in years. It's a winding, uphill road that just got narrower the more we climbed.

"Naw? Well, the way Dad and Cynthia talk about you, you could have fooled me."

I guess I did kind of have that good-girl stereotype. I didn't get the honor of being voted Class Slut, but I wasn't named Biggest Bookworm either.

"I got a B in AP Physics," I said, a hint of sarcasm coming out. "It was really hard."

Luke laughed and I knew that he got my humor. "Why would AP Physics be hard?" he joked.

"Beats me," I said, "it's so straightforward."

The '67 Rover took another turn and I could see the landscape changing. The trees were thinning out as we approached the top of the hill, and the wide blue sky was opening up before us.

"So your boyfriend must be bummed he didn't get into your Ivy League, huh?"

Ha. Very clever. I just laughed.

"Oh no, you dumped him and broke his heart, right after prom? How could you?" Luke whistled real low.

I turned to look at Luke with an open-mouth rebuttal. "Sorry, I don't do psycho boy games."

"Wait, wait, I got it," he continued. "You're going to string him along with the long-distance thing for the first half of freshman year until you both get settled, then, bam, you're going to kick him to the curb!" Luke carefully pulled into Mattamuskee Bluff's dirt parking lot and parked under the clump of trees that were dead center. "Am I right or am I right?" He was nodding like a stand-up comic.

He was nowhere near right. There was no mad-cool senior-year boyfriend for me to break up with before college. There was no boy back home pining away for me. But I wasn't pining away for anyone there either.

So that was something.

"Does it make you happy to tease me?" I said in my

best fake-irritated voice.

Luke hopped out of the Land Rover and unbuckled Hunter. He smiled at me. "Very happy."

I reached around to fasten Rosy into the baby carrier on my chest. It was funny how much easier it was to have another person helping with the kids.

"What about you? Does it make you happy when I tease you?" Luke asked me as he held Hunter's hand. We walked away from the Land Rover and toward the bluff.

"Oh yeah, it warms the cockles of my heart," I said back.

Luke snorted, and I focused on the trail ahead.

We reached the edge of Mattamuskee Bluff where a big stone plaque proclaimed its discovery and preservation. A cliff walk teetered along the edge of the bluff with an uneven fence alongside it. Straight below were pointed rocks with waves crashing against them. Beyond our high outcropping was the winding, uneven coast, dotted with houses and rocky cliffs.

I opened my eyes to the bright sunshine and saw the cloud-streaked sky before me. The ocean was enormous and wild before us. The splash of the waves against the rocks was a steady sound, calming and nerve-wracking all at once.

"Watch your step," Luke said, looking back at me as we walked single file on the trail.

The views were amazing. The vastness of the water. The heat of the sun. My adrenaline was pumping from being up so high. Sometimes our sandals would catch on some loose rocks and a spray of sand would go trickling down the edge of the cliff through the gaps in the wire fencing that was tacked up. To protect us from falling? My heart raced a little as Hunter manipulated the trail. We went slow, real slow, and Luke held on to Hunter's hand very tightly. The sun was beating down on us and I was glad I had dressed Rosy in loose-fitting pj's that covered her skin. A big floppy sun hat shielded her face as she rested on my chest, a warm breathing thing sucking on a plug.

I liked the fact that we were hiking because it reminded me of home. I missed my parents, Steph, even my brother Ben's obnoxious electric-guitar playing. I missed them more than I had other years because I knew I would only be returning for a week, and then the big move: college.

The trail widened a bit and we could spread out a little and walk side by side. Hunter was walking up on a grassy spot away from the edge.

Luke gestured to the ocean with his arm, "Nothing beats kayaking the waves."

I snorted. "Ditto. My thoughts exactly."

Luke laughed. "So fill me in, April. What's been going on in the life of Mattamuskee's favorite nanny?" Luke was talking all game-show-esque but he actually seemed interested.

"Oh, you know," I started. "Just the basics. Saving the sea turtles, ending world hunger, that sort of thing."

Luke smiled. "I know what you do in your *free time*, but tell me what you've been up to in . . . what's the name of that little town you come from? Backasswardville?"

"Hey!" I exclaimed, motioning to Hunter.

"What's BlackAxWordVille?" Hunter asked, trotting along in the grass.

"Slow down, Hunt," I said, "remember, we stay together when we walk, right?"

"Right," he said like a dejected video-game loser.

I turned to Luke and gave him an imaginary bullet to

the middle of his forehead.

"What was that?" he said after my facial expression went back to normal.

"Let's just say it was invisible and it rhymes with the words nine billibeter."

"Ouch!" Luke said. Then he reached for Hunter's hand. "Okay, go real slow at this part. Bend your knees and keep your weight low."

The trail had narrowed again and we were heading down a steepish hill. I held Rosy close to me and felt the rocks underneath my feet. If I fell forward I would land on her. If I slipped backward I would have very little to hold on to. I started to feel the earth move around me so I sat down. Luke noticed right away.

"Are you okay?" he asked, clinging to Hunter as we were stopped mid-path.

I shook my head. "I don't think this is such a good idea with the kids." I looked at Hunter's disappointed face.

"But I want to see 'ffiti rock again!" he whined.

I raised an eyebrow at Luke.

Luke said, "He means graffiti. Not *bad* graffiti. It's just a big peace sign."

"You've taken him here before?"

Hunter nodded vigorously. "Lukey put my letters on the rock. I want to see if they're still there! It's an H and an R. Those are my letters. H and R for Hunter and Rogers."

Luke had defaced a piece of nature for the sake of looking cool to a four-year-old? Oh *my* God. He was the *anti-nanny-manual*.

I stood up and shook my nerves free. "Well, you never said anything about a peace sign. Heck yeah, show me where it's at."

It wasn't until that instant that I realized one thing. I was completely in *like* with Luke Rogers. Well, for at least another three hours until I told Cynthia and Doug about our lie and got his butt the heck out of my job.

We traveled over the winding, rocky trail for another fifteen minutes until we got to a cool lookout point with a massive natural rock. There it was in all its glory. A big old peace sign painted white, surrounded by tons of other tags and hearts with names inside them, and way over on a far corner, a little H.R. etched into the rock.

Hunter was sitting in Luke's lap munching down a banana (a real one, not invisible), and I was propped under a sort-of shady tree giving Rosy a bottle, when my phone went off. I was a little startled to have the real world sneak up on me while we were up atop this awesome cliff. Being up so high was exhilarating. Just being away from the noise of cars and people and other people's kids screaming.

Up there at the top of Mattamuskee Bluff it was just the repetitive *crash, crash, crash* of the waves hitting the rocks. There were long stretches of quiet in between waves, and then *crash,* a big one would hit so hard it would send sprays of white foam up into the air.

I opened my phone and saw a text waiting from Cynthia. It was the day's grocery list. Sometimes she would ask me to send an instant pic back to her so she could see what the kids were doing at that exact moment. I squinted my eyes as I read the text and hoped she didn't ask for one now. I quickly scanned through part of the list: org strwberrs, ched chees, nacho chips, grass fed beef, deli pot salad. And, then, there it was, drat: *What R my babes up to?*

Well, here goes nothing, I thought. I angled the phone down at Rosy and snapped a picture of her sucking down her bottle. After it registered I hit send. It was pretty much just a close-up of her face so Cynthia wouldn't be able to tell we were hanging out at make-out point, or rather, Mattamuskee's pot-smoking spot for the young and the jobless. I looked over at Luke and Hunter by the big peace sign. Hunter was tossing his banana peel over the edge. I shook my head. No time like the present.

"Smile!" I said, aiming the phone at them.

"It's biode*grabe*able!" Hunter exclaimed, tossing the other banana peel over.

I clicked a shot and in that instant the phone went dead. We were out of batteries.

We were way behind schedule. Hunter's lunch ended up being an energy bar and a juice box in the Land Rover on the way to the grocery store, and I realized that if Hunter didn't actually get a real rest before swim class, then he might actually have a meltdown in the pool. We were rushing through the grocery store—Luke had Rosy strapped onto him and was pushing the shopping cart with Hunter in it (rest time) while I darted around the store grabbing items.

It was taking me extra time to read my grocery list since the phone was dead. I'd had to plug in the phone in the car lighter and jot down the list on an old receipt while the fifty-year-old Land Rover bumped down the windy Cliff Drive.

Because Luke's vehicle didn't even have a *windshield*, let alone windows to roll up, the little scrap of paper kept flapping in the breeze and my handwriting was more like baby scrawl.

"Does that say grass-fed beef or grass-wheat drink?" I murmured out loud.

Luke was enjoying it all a little too much.

He tracked me like a deer in the cross hairs, following closely with the cart and making comments, like, "Score two points, April. The raisins are on sale."

"Would you just watch where you're going?" I said. "You almost ran over my flip flop."

"What, were you a hall monitor up through twelfth grade?" He grinned and waited for me to smack him.

I refused.

I looked at Luke and smiled. "I was a total hall monitor."

"Sweet!" He raised his hand for a high five. "Hall monitors are hot!"

I returned the high five, and he clasped my hand and brought it down. "Seriously, April, you are one cool hall monitor." He was looking right at me like I was the only girl in the grocery store. His face had changed and he was trying to show me that all the teasing was just boy-speak for "I like you."

"Wow, thanks, you sound just like my fourth-grade boyfriend."

Luke didn't care about the diss. He was just smiling away. Not letting go of my hand. Letting the other shoppers stream past us with their carts filled up. "Umm, checkout?" I said, letting go of his hand and trying to have less tunnel vision.

"Totally," he said.

All through checkout he was just as happy as a clam. Putting the groceries on the revolving belt, bagging them in our reusable bags printed with the pretty pastel earth pictures, holding Rosy as he loaded them back into the shopping cart. I swiped the Rogers' credit card through the machine, and Luke didn't even ask me to buy him a chocolate bar. I shook my head as I thought how Luke was really a natural at this "manny" thing. Maybe I had underestimated him. I had been known to veto potential boys back at home before they could even get the chance to ask me out.

I checked my watch. Okay. We were cutting it close, but if we didn't hit any midday traffic through town, I would have fifteen minutes to put away groceries and set Hunter up with his watercolors before we had to get ready for swim class.

Luke was tickling Rosy's feet in her cloth baby booties while she was still strapped to his chest, so I pushed the full cart of groceries as we exited the grocery store. Hunter was walking in between us and holding on to the side of the shopping cart.

As we started walking across the parking lot to the far right corner, I gave Luke a sideways glance. He was, I decided, definitely not worth vetoing. Yet.

I put on my smart-aleck voice and said, "You know, I got into Harvard, but I'm not going there."

He gave me a quick jaw drop. "No way."

"Way," I said, giving my head a little shake so my long hair flirted with the breeze. I hadn't noticed it before, but Luke had this adorable mole right on his neck. As he walked, it peeked out from under the neck of his T-shirt. Same side as that big snakey tattoo. Our day out in the sun had given him this raw scent. I breathed it in.

"Umm, why aren't you going to Harvard, dumbass?" he said, smiling but not looking at me.

When he walked, his posture was confident and forward-moving. Just like mine. I took a deeper stride as I prepared my answer.

"Okay, you can chill on the *expletives*. And why am I not going to Harvard? One reason: money. I didn't get the scholarship I'd hoped for."

Luke nodded.

He was really a lot hotter today than he was yesterday. Go figure.

"So, you know," I started, thinking I might try to initiate a little spark. "I noticed that snake tattoo on your arm?"

"Yeah?" I could see him grinning, but he didn't make eye contact.

"Uh-huh. What's that all about? Is it a boa? I have this friend back home who –"

Luke took a broad step and yelled out, "Hunter!" His voice was an urgent boom. "Stop!"

I glanced down to my side and saw that Hunter was not holding on to the shopping cart anymore.

Then as I looked up everything went into slow-motion.

I saw Luke taking two long bounds forward with baby Rosy strapped to his chest.

Watching him was like watching a frame-by-frame movie. I was frozen to my spot.

A fast second later, Luke reached Hunter, who had skipped ahead of us.

I held my breath.

Luke grabbed Hunter's arm roughly, pulling him back.

In the next instant, a big red SUV backed out of a parking spot and was directly in front them, missing hitting Hunter by a hair.

I stood there, a few feet back, and squeezed the handle of the shopping cart. My heart was racing.

The man driving the SUV, who looked to be about sixty and friendly enough, was talking with a bluetooth. He didn't immediately realize that he had almost hit Hunter with his car.

As I rushed up to them, Luke was motioning with his hands for the man to roll down his window.

"You almost ran him over!" Luke said to the man. The man peered down to where Hunter was and his face flashed embarrassed and apologetic.

"I didn't see him, sorry," the man said weakly as he shrugged and backed up, superslow now.

Luke shook his head. "Watch where you're going!" he shouted at him as the man drove away. Luke shook his anger off and turned to Hunter. "You okay, bud?"

Hunter nodded, seemingly oblivious to the situation.

But I stood there stunned. How could I have not been watching? How could I have let this happen?

Hunter did not have a meltdown at swim practice. I did.

I sat there alone on the bench, sticking Rosy's pacifier back in her mouth every time she spit it out, and replayed the parking lot scene over and over in my head.

One second he was trotting alongside me, the obedient little boy that he was, and the next instant he was two parking spaces ahead, almost getting run over. Knocked to the ground? Killed? It was all too horrible to consider. But these things did happen. When Hunter painted his watercolor before swim class, I had googled "kids getting run over by SUVs." I didn't click on any of the graphic videos posted of people getting run over, but I did see an article that said a child *survived* getting run over by her parent. That made me a feel a little better. But not much.

Hunter was an amazing boy. And he relied on me for everything. Like keeping him safe and not letting him get killed and stuff.

I had already taken him grocery shopping a handful of times. He had never skipped ahead. He had always stayed right by my side asking me an endless battery of questions.

But I hadn't been talking to him this time. I had been talking to Luke.

I relived the moment when Luke called out Hunter's name, when he took the fast leaps to reach his side, and when he pulled Hunter back by his shoulder. Hunter hadn't looked scared at Luke's roughness, or angry, or anything. He had just turned around, confused. I don't think he fully understood what had just happened. How a one-second moment could change your life forever.

Luke and I had started a conversation about it during the car ride home.

"That's how fast something can happen," I said, still stunned. "Just like that."

Luke was visibly upset by the whole thing. "I know, that was really scary. I knew I shouldn't have let him get ahead. But he's just so independent."

I hadn't even *noticed* that he had gotten ahead. How bad was that? I looked at Luke's snake tattoo as he drove us home and cringed.

When he pulled up to the curb to let us out, I put my hand on his arm and said, "Thank you." I shook my head in apology.

"Hey, you would have done the same thing I did," he said.

I shook my head again. The difference was: I hadn't.

I opened the Land Rover door and got out. Luke let Hunter out and started transferring the car seats back into the garage. Hunter ran up onto the porch and found a new animal magazine that had come in the mail for him. He sat down and promptly started leafing through it. I waited for Luke by the driver's side of his vehicle.

When he came back and saw me there with Rosy on my hip, he pulled me into a hug. This was not what I was expecting. I thought by now it may have dawned on him how negligent I was back at the parking lot. He could have been mad at me, disappointed, anything. *I* was mad at me—and definitely disappointed. But all of the sudden we were standing in the street, and Luke had has arms around me like he was a giant brown bear.

Rosy was being gently sandwiched between us as Luke just squeezed his body around mine. He was sort of clinging to me, releasing his breath in one long sigh. I let myself go for a second. Just a second to release.

"Oh, April, that was bad," he said, but he meant the incident, not my role in it. I could feel how much he loved Hunter more than I did, how being here wasn't just an escape from a bad internship, but a chance to come home. And how we had almost just screwed everything up.

"It won't happen again," I said. "I'll be more careful."

Luke loosened his arms and looked at me. "If I hadn't been here today, distracting you guys, getting you off-routine...."

I quickly shook my head. "No. I am the one responsible for them, not you. I wasn't paying attention. *You* saved us."

Luke released us from the hug and I glanced over my shoulder at Hunter. He was busy looking at the magazine. "Look, Luke, I think you should come clean to Doug and Cynthia. I think it would make everything around here a little easier."

He stiffened. "*Wait.* I thought we were cool."

The image of Hunter almost being flattened by that car flashed in my mind. "We are, we are. I mean, just for Hunter's sake. So he doesn't have to go on lying." *Or me . . .*

Luke shook his head and bolted for the front of the house. He kneeled down to Hunter, and as I walked slowly after him, pacing my steps in extra slow time, I could tell he was sealing the secret deal again. Luke stood up when I approached and gave me puppy dog eyes. "I'll see you in a couple days, okay?" he said.

"How about tomorrow?" I suggested.

"Tomorrow I have an interview in Providence. *For a new internship.* I am going to tell my dad and Cynthia after that, okay?"

My head was fuzzing up. "Okay?"

He nodded and went to peck me on the cheek. But it kind of slid over and got part of my mouth. And it sort of lingered there for a second. Then he rushed over to his Rover and got in. As he pulled away he gave a small salute. I stood there on the doorstep like a fool. Had Luke Rogers just kissed me?

I just hoped Cynthia wouldn't show up at swim practice to see my double meltdown.

Thank God it was pizza night. Not take-out, but the easy kind made at home with a pre-baked crust, sauce out of a jar, and lots of fresh mozzarella and veggies thrown on top. I kept my back to Doug and Cynthia when they entered the kitchen. They didn't seem to notice.

Cynthia had left a note that she was taking a long bath before dinner (she was a no-show at swim practice) and Doug had rolled in at the usual train time.

I had put a bottle of red wine on the table—a bold move not indicated in the nanny manual. But today was all about bold moves.

Being their daytime nanny, I didn't have to eat dinner with them because I was technically off-duty, but after a long day with the kids and then cooking all the food for dinner, it was impossible to not sit down and chow. Even on that day.

The Accident

I was at the kitchen counter helping myself to some salad with croutons when Cynthia circled the table that Hunter and I had set.

"Wine?" she said, and then, "are you going to eat with us?"

I turned around and looked at her sheepishly. "Is that okay?"

She came over and patted my back. Her short spiky hair smelled like fruit shampoo. "Of course it is! We love to have you eat with us, but we don't want you to feel like you *have* to."

"I know." Cynthia did really have a warm side that reminded me of home. When she wasn't checking for dust on the shelves. Or throwing out perfectly good yogurt because it was due to expire in a week.

Doug pulled the pizza stone out of the oven and slid the pie onto a cutting board. Cynthia went over, gave him a little kiss on the cheek, and got some wine glasses out of the cabinet. They were just milling about the kitchen island in the most normal of ways, but all I could think was: Your son almost died today.

Hunter sat next to me at the table and I patted his knee.

Cynthia looked at me from the kitchen. "Do you want a glass of wine, April?" she asked.

I sat there dumbstruck for a second. "Uhh . . . no thanks," I said hesitantly.

She cocked her head. "Are you sure? The drinking age in Europe is eighteen. I'm not encouraging you to break the law, but at the same time, a glass of wine isn't going to kill you." She laughed. "This is the doctor speaking!" She was definitely in one of her no-C-section-day moods. An easy day at work. Or she was acting like a cool aunt who goes against what your mother would say. This must have been one of those opposites-attract things that made Cynthia and my mom best friends. My mom would enjoy a glass of wine now and again but she would never offer *us* one.

"It's actually good for your heart," Doug chimed in as he cut the pizza into slices.

Seeing as my heart was breaking with the weight of that SUV parked inside it, I tilted my head at Cynthia. "Umm, okay. A little glass, then," I said.

She smiled. "Just as long as we can toast you." She poured three glasses on the counter and held one up. "To a job well done. I know how hard it is to take care of children."

She had no idea.

The pizza and the wine made it to the table, along with a sleeping Rosy (off-schedule) in her portable swing. I took a big sip of the wine and forced it down. It tasted bitter and warm and I almost gagged. I added a bit of water to my glass and washed the taste away with some salad. I didn't have a super ton of experience with alcohol so I took a bite of mushroom-and-green-pepper-topped pizza and glugged another mouthful of wine. It burned my throat as it went down but I was starting to feel a buzzing tingly feeling in my head.

"So what's going on with Luke?" Cynthia asked Doug, out of the blue.

I literally gagged on my food and almost spewed a chunk of cheese on the table.

"Are you all right, April?" Doug asked.

I nodded and got up to go beat my chest and cough up my lung in the kitchen.

Oh my God. I was a walking cliché.

I filled a glass with water and downed it.

When I came back to the table they were still talking about Luke.

"What do you mean you haven't heard if he's coming to my speech on Thursday?" Cynthia whined. "It's in Boston after all!"

Doug cleared his throat. "I told you. I did hear. I just *said* he sent an e-mail asking what time it was."

"That doesn't mean he's coming."

"He's coming." Doug tried to end the conversation.

"This is Luke we're talking about here," Cynthia said. "It's not like he's got the greatest track record."

Doug gave her evil dart eyes.

Cynthia ignored him and seemed oblivious to me hanging on her words. "I mean it's one thing to make the dean's list, honey, but it's another entirely to get into repeated trouble with the law."

Trouble with the law? I swallowed hard.

Doug was getting annoyed. "You know the cops in Boston are like no others. They never bothered us as much as they bother college students today."

Cynthia rolled her eyes, took a forkful of pizza, and then looked at me. "Good pizza. You sure do take after your mother."

I raised the wine to my lips to finish it. "Sure do," I said.

Then I stared at the pizza, my mind on autowhirl, and said, "So what's that about Luke? Did you say he made dean's list?"

Oh. My. God. What was wrong with me?

Cynthia forked some of her mesclun greens. "Yes, he did. He's on a brand-new career path," she said sarcastically. "He's going to be a research scientist this summer!"

Or not.

Doug looked pointedly at me and said, "Luke finished in the top five in his physics class at BU. He's pulling himself together this year."

"Is he now?" Cynthia snorted.

"I'm going to BC," I said, trying to change the subject. "I got a full scholarship."

Cynthia winked her wrinkles at me. "I know. We couldn't be happier for you."

I glanced down at Hunter, who was munching away on his food, and felt a mix of guilt for lying about Luke and relief that it would all soon be over. The important thing was that Hunter was alive. Content. I was going to BC in the fall. Luke would fess up soon enough and maybe at the next family dinner he'd be joining us for sushi take-out night. Maybe no one would ever have to know that Hunter had almost been run over in the supermarket parking lot.

Cynthia wasn't letting up on the Luke-bashing. "I swear to you, Doug, if that boy doesn't check in with us this summer, I don't know what I am going to do," Cynthia said. "All I do is worry about him. More than his own mother."

What the?

Doug sighed out, annoyed.

"Luke is . . ." Hunter started. "Luke is. . . ."

I looked at him. Oh yeah. Here came Luke out of the closet. I tried to give Hunter mental telepathy by repeating "Go, Hunter, go, Hunter, go" in my head. Hunter caught my eye and we shared a look. Then he smiled.

"Luke's da best brother ever," Hunter said.

"Did you hear that?" Doug said, thumbing down to Hunter. "Honey, what more could you ask for?"

Cynthia was in no mood to concede. She popped another forkful of pizza in her mouth and said, "Role modeling, anyone?"

Doug rolled his eyes.

"Hunter, why is Luke the best big brother? What does

he do that makes him so special?" Cynthia asked.

Hunter started squirming in his seat. A few answers came to my mind. He was super hot; he was funny; he saved the kid's life . . .

Hunter looked at the calendar and saw the circled red day. "Umm," he said, totally in control, "Luke knows how to build really cool things with Legos."

"Exactly!" Doug clapped his hands together. "Point taken!"

I let my eyes wander over to the living room where a Lego car was resting atop an end table. I made a mental note to move that to the playroom later. I wasn't exactly a whiz with the Legos. I thought of Luke and that hug. I had never been hugged like that before. By a guy. In the middle of the street. In the middle of the day. Luke had this side of him that I wished I had in myself. It was a side that didn't care what the world thought, a side that would attempt to kiss my cheek and let it "accidentally" land on my mouth, a side that wanted to break the rules. I had always buried that side of myself.

"April," Cynthia said, breaking me out of my reverie. "Your note from the other day on the white board—I keep forgetting to ask you."

I spun my head around and reread my words, *Can we chat about a visitor??* And Cynthia's scrawled reply: *Yes!*

Luke. Visiting. For how long?

"Yeah," I said, "about that . . ."

Cynthia got up and started clearing the plates. "Yes?" she said.

I had a sudden and immediate urge to conceal the truth about my note on the message board. I didn't want to tell them about Luke in the basement, and have it lead to telling about him saving Hunter's life. I wanted to start over. But how? With just another small lie?

"Umm, I was wondering if my friend Steph from home could come visit one weekend I have off? And stay here?"

Cynthia smiled warmly. "Absolutely."

I thanked her and got up. I went to the white board and used a cloth to erase the message. Problem solved.

TWO DAYS AFTER THE ACCIDENT

Steph threw her stuff in the back of the silver Volvo wagon and got in the passenger side. Rosy was falling asleep from just being placed in the car seat, her head bobbing into her chest, and I had given Hunter a device to keep his attention off of our conversation.

Steph glanced over her shoulder at the kids, and in an agitated whisper, said, "What's going on?"

I pulled out of the Rogerses' driveway and headed down toward the bus station.

I avoided her eyes and checked on Hunter. He had the ear buds in and was immersed in Teenage Mutant Ninja Turtles.

"What do you mean what's going on?" I whispered.

She brought her face real close to mine. "There's something you're not telling me. I can feel it," she said.

I tried to look innocent. No, that was too obvious. I tried to look unconcerned. That was not working either.

I just had to make it to the bus station and drop her

off without losing it. I tried to change the subject.

"Yeah, there's a lot I haven't told you about me and Luke. But none of it matters right now," I said.

"Are you *sure*?" She was staring at me.

I drove the car slow and steady, feeling the road beneath the tires like it could be pulled out from under us at any moment. "Look. I feel like I'm going insane. Okay? I am sorry that I dragged you to that party. If I hadn't, none of this would have happened. Luke wouldn't be in the hospital. And Ollie wouldn't be dead."

Steph stopped me. "Not so fast. What are you saying?"

I pleaded her with my eyes and my emotion went into overdrive. "Don't you see? It's all. My. Fault."

"Oh. My. God." Steph sat back in her seat and closed her eyes. "It is so not your fault."

"Yeah, see, I knew you would say that. Believe that, even. That's what you are supposed to say! But if you really think about, if I hadn't brought you to the party, you wouldn't have been hooking up with Ollie, and he wouldn't have tried to take you off to some place, who knows where, and the whole thing wouldn't have happened." I clutched the steering wheel and checked Hunter in the rear view mirror. Fully engrossed.

Steph spoke in exasperation.

"First of all, if you put it that way, then you're saying that it's all *my* fault! But it's not, April! It's not mine and it's not yours. Okay? But I do take responsibility for my own PDA that night. All those beers were beyond stupid. But *I* drank them. Nobody forced them down my throat. And I was the one getting down on the couch with Ollie." She snorted a little. "I'd love to give you credit for that one, but sorry, you can't be a martyr here either. I knew what I was doing."

"How can you argue with me? You don't even

remember what happened."

"I remember enough."

Did she know I was covering for Luke? Had she figured me out?

We pulled into the bus station parking lot and I was overcome by an impending feeling of loss. Steph put her hand on mine and said, "I hear ya, April. I am so sorry. But friends are supposed to push each other to be better people. I just want you to *talk* to me."

"I can't."

Steph squeezed me and said, "You will. *Please?*" She was about to cry. "I promise I will support you. No matter what happens." She rushed out of the car and went to get her bag in the back. I got out and stood by the driver's side door. "Don't say good-bye," she said, on the verge of tears. "Just call me tonight."

I nodded and put my hand up for a silent farewell.

And then she was gone.

When I got back in the car, the cell phone was sounding to let me know I had a message. I checked the voicemail. It was Doug. I listened to his message by holding the phone away from my ear. He was talking loud.

"April. Doug. I just got a call from your lawyer. You can stop by the police station when it's convenient to pick up your bag. We had a little chat. The cops have no further questions at this time. It's a goddamn media firestorm out there about the emergency response time. So I think they are laying low for a while until that dies down. Lest any other mistakes get brought to light. Anyway, he said your initial statement was very comprehensive, and he knows to call Diane, your lawyer, first if he needs to talk to you.

Okay. That's it. Remember, if he tries to get you to talk, don't. He said they have no further questions at this time. Take care."

I shut the phone. It was now or never. I turned the ignition and headed toward the police station.

I tried to calm my nerves. Okay, so everyone who was questioned at the party said they saw Ollie driving. And they gave the same story as I did about Luke getting pulled into the car, and Steph being passed out, and me trying to get help but being squelched. Okay, so I didn't need to be so paranoid. I just had to make it through picking up my bag, looking confident and unafraid, and I could leave. Soon enough, I would be saying good-bye to Mattamuskee, Rhode Island, anyway, and would be able to put this all behind me. I just had to hold it together at the station and give them no reason to doubt me.

When I pulled into the police department parking lot, Rosy was still asleep. I unbuckled Hunter, turned off his device, and stored it in the glove box. Then I lifted a sleeping Rosy out of her seat and settled her on my shoulder. She kept sleeping. I locked the car doors and took Hunter's hand.

"Where are we going?" he asked.

I smiled brightly. "You get to see a real police station!"

His eyes opened wide. "Yes!"

"Yes!" I echoed. Truly it was a joy for both of us.

"Will they show me their guns?" Hunter asked.

"Oh, I sure hope so," I said.

He didn't pick up the sarcasm.

It felt good to loosen up a bit from all the heavy feelings.

"And the jail cell?" Hunter said, walking faster to the front door.

"If you're lucky, someday you *will* see the inside of a

jail cell."

"Wow! Cool!"

I opened the door. Having him along definitely calmed my nerves.

The female cop behind the front counter looked us over as we walked in. "Wow, cool!" Hunter said. "A mommy cop!"

She didn't look amused.

"Okay, calm down. First I have to get my bag, all right, then maybe you can ask one question."

"May I help you?" the not-a-mommy cop asked.

I cleared my throat, trying not to disturb the sleeping Rosy on my shoulder. "My name is April Nichols. I've come to collect my bag."

"Have a seat and Morris will be out in a minute."

Oh God. Why couldn't she just give me my bag?

Hunter leaped over to the waiting area and grabbed a mug shot book. It was the start of a thousand questions. "What is this book? Who are these people? Why are they grumpy? Why doesn't he have a shirt on? Why is there brothers on here?"

I started to explain things to him. "These are called mug shots. When you do something bad and get arrested, the police take your picture. These are all bad guys."

"Bad guys, cool!"

The female cop looked over at us, annoyed. What? The kid asked me eight thousand questions a day. If I didn't start explaining the world to him, I'd be depriving him. If he was old enough to understand it, he was old enough to hear it. I think . . .

A few minutes later, Colonel Morris came out and extended a warm hand. I shook it and Rosy stirred upon hearing his deep voice, but she didn't wake up.

"Come this way," he said, and we followed him down

a hall.

Hunter raced to catch up to Colonel Morris. "Can I see the jail?" he asked.

Not a shy one, that boy.

Colonel Morris laughed. Then he leaned over and put his hands on his knees. "Do you want to go inside?"

Hunter nodded excitedly.

"And lock you in?" Colonel Morris said.

Hunter looked at me. "Umm . . ."

I smiled. "He'll let you out. I'll be right there watching."

Hunter looked up at the cop. "Okay. Can you lock her in, too?"

This time I was the one who was saying "Umm . . ." as we went to get my bag. He handed it to me and asked me to check the contents to see if anything was missing. I opened the plastic bag and attempted to go through my purse with one hand.

"Yeah, it's all in there," I said. Baby wipes, a diaper, sunglasses, keys, wallet, sunblock stick, paper, pen, tampon, floss, a few stray crayons.

"Great," he said. "So what's your name, little guy?"

Hunter instantly scowled. "I'm not little."

"Oh, well, of course not. That was a test. Let me try again. What's your name, big guy?"

"Hunter."

Colonel Morris bellowed, again stirring Rosy. "Whoah, that's a powerful name! Hunter. My goodness."

He led us to the holding cells. I prayed no one was in any.

Luckily, they were empty.

"Here you go, big guy," Richard said, opening one.

Hunter went cautiously inside. "Whoah," he said, checking out the bars and then the toilet. "Real bad guys go in here?"

"The worst bad guys," Richard said.

Okay, lovely.

"Like bank robbers?" Hunter asked.

Colonel Morris nodded slow. "Oh, yeah, lots of bank robbers."

And rapists. And murderers. And drunk drivers who killed their friends by accident. Fun times.

"Go ahead, check it out," Richard was saying as Hunter examined the steel bed. He climbed on it and tried it out. Richard swung the door shut, but not locked, and looked at me.

"So I've got one question for you."

I patted Rosy's back. Thought: Use her as a shield. Wake her up. Pinch her. Make her cry. But I just kept patting her nervously. "Oh yeah? What's that?"

Colonel Morris looked into my eyes. "Do you trust me?"

Gulp. Huh? Did I trust myself anymore?

"Uh, yeah," I said. Did this count as answering questions?

"Well, let me tell you. I've been on the force for thirty-five years. And I've seen a lot of accidents. I've seen this town change from a small, working-class blue collar town to a suburb filled with high-priced houses and commuters. I've seen highway accidents, back road accidents."

Hunter was walking his feet up the wall of the jail cell bed. Richard ignored him and continued.

"I've even seen an accident in that very same spot. But I've never seen an accident where the vehicle didn't have a windshield. And I've never seen an accident where two guys were ejected from a car and only one survived. And I've never seen one where two girls in the back come away without a scratch and there is only one person with any recollection of the entire event. I've seen a lot of things in my time, but this one is nagging at me."

"April, look!" Hunter said, now standing on the bed and jumping off.

I smiled my "no, no" smile at Hunter, hoping Richard would intercede, but he just kept on spewing. "Look. It's nothing I can explain, right here, right now. But I want you to know that if you have something to tell me, you can. *You can trust me.* I can sit on it awhile until you leave your job here. I can wait until you're on your way home, the Baker family has come and gone and said their good-byes. I know the law, but I also know how people operate. Things come out."

I squeezed Rosy in my arms and looked at him. "Yes," I said. "I appreciate that."

"Is there something you want to tell me now, off the record?"

I shook my head. "I've told you everything."

He looked me in the eyes. I looked away. I was shaking in my skin, but I was almost done.

"Hunter, come on out," I said.

Hunter obeyed immediately. For once.

"Say thank you," I said.

"Thank you!"

Colonel Morris smiled and was back to being jolly Santa. He leaned over with his hands on his knees and said, "You're very welcome, young man. You come back any time."

Yeah, I'm sure Doug will plan a field trip.

"Okay!" Hunter squealed.

Richard looked up at me, his belly bulging over his pants. "Sure you don't want to give it a look?" he said, motioning to the jail cell.

I shook my head, smiled to get the nerves away, and

took Hunter's hand as we prepared to leave.

I looked at Colonel Morris and thought, I don't trust you *that* much.

I wish I had said the same to Luke.

FIVE WEEKS BEFORE THE ACCIDENT

I couldn't help myself. I had to go there. Rosy was down for a morning nap, so I snapped the baby monitor to the elastic waist of my terry-cloth short shorts and grabbed Hunter's hand.

"We're going on a treasure hunt!" I exclaimed.

"Where?" he said, instantaneously thrilled.

"To the basement!" I said with all the theater I could muster.

"To find what?" he played along.

Luke? An answer? A reason to slow down this speeding train that was my brain?

"Umm . . . ," I said. "Cobwebs . . . a stray nail . . . maybe even a water heater!"

"A water heater!" Hunter said, jumping up. "What's a water heater!?"

I looked at him with spooky eyes and said in a maniacal voice, "That is for yooouuu to find out!" I seriously hoped Luke didn't have an extra monitor down there so he could spy on us. "Onward, young captain!" I said as Hunter bolted for the sliding glass doors.

For a second, as I shut the sliding glass doors, I thought it was bad karma to leave Rosy unattended up on the third floor. Conceivably, someone could come and snatch her away if they had been watching our every move. Or maybe she'd wake up crying and the monitor wouldn't work from as far away as we were roaming. I shook off my nervousness and thought, *We'll only be down there for a minute. Until we drag Luke upstairs.*

The outdoor entrance to the basement consisted of two metal doors painted grey, on a slant from the edge of the house. I stood on one and pulled on the other. It was open. Hunter and I carefully walked down the stairs, leaving the metal door open. I felt for a string hanging from the first light bulb and pulled it.

"I spot cobwebs!" Hunter said, jumping up to point them out.

"That's one!" I said. "What was next?"

It wasn't so bad down there.

"A nail!" he squealed, plunging ahead into the darkness.

What was wrong with my nannying instincts? Was I actually sending him on a search for a rusty nail to poke himself with? I pulled another light bulb string, expecting to see Luke materialize in the glow of it.

The first area had a freezer, an extra fridge, and an industrial sink. We walked around some support poles to get to the other side of the basement. The furnaces, an old pool table, seasonal stuff like skis and kid toys. I pulled a couple more light bulb strings. It looked completely unoccupied.

"Hello?" I said.

Nothing.

Where had Luke been sleeping? That old, ratty plaid couch in the corner?

"Who are you calling?" Hunter asked.

"Umm, are you there, *Water Heater*?" I said.

"I know!" He stuck his finger up in the air like a detective and went back to the first section. I poked around the shelves and miscellaneous stuff, but I couldn't find Luke's frame pack or sleeping bag stashed anywhere. The monitor on my waist crackled as it struggled to keep range with its digital sidekick upstairs.

Then I heard hammering. Quiet at first, then louder. I walked toward the basement entrance and found Hunter hammering a pipe underneath the sink.

"I think I found the water heater!" he said, happily clacking away. I bent down and touched the hammer before he could wield another deadly blow.

"Let's not break it. This is called a pipe. It doesn't heat the water. It lets the water drain down into it when you're done using the water." *Where was Luke?*

"Oh," Hunter said, dejected. He put the hammer back into the tool box he had opened up and grabbed the measuring tape. Then he brightened. "What does it look like? Maybe I could measure it!"

"It's round but not like a ball. It's tall and curved like this," I said, making a cylinder with my arms. "I'll give you a hint. It's white and made of metal."

Hunter went scampering off to examine all corners of the basement, believing that speed helped solve the riddle.

Speed and determination—a boy's best friends.

I found a pencil and a piece of scrap paper in the tool box, so I wrote a quick note while Hunter worked.

Text me tonight after 6. No lie—we need to talk.

Then I put my cell phone number on it. I rested the paper on the first place Luke might see it. On top of the freezer near the doors. I weighed it down with the stray nail Hunter had scored.

"Hunt, you ready?" I called, walking around and flicking off the lights.

He had scrambled to the entrance again and was standing proudly next to the water heater. The measuring tape was wrapped around it three times.

"Good job," I said, cringing inwardly. "You found it."

"I went *fast*," he said, pleased with his knots.

I nodded. "Most boys do."

My dad has this annoying habit of blowing air through his mouth like a horse flapping its lips. Loudly. Like a balloon deflating. If my dad, out in the rolling, green hills of our home, is faced with a particularly difficult tree removal, or if he is suspended from ropes and dangling under the threat of a tree limb about to fall, he will hold his breath, and, when everything is clear again, he'll let out a big, motor-boat-sounding gum flap. I hate this.

It's a stress reliever, he says.

It's a stress reliever, I told myself, as I walked out of the Rogers' house and down their path. I let out a big sigh and my lips vibrated with the exhalation. Just like Dad.

Luke had texted me at 6:05.

Wassup?

I texted back: *Can we meet?*

He replied: *My place or yours?* (Winking smile emoji.)

I returned the winking smile.

He texted directions to an apartment. A ten-minute walk.

I waved to Doug and Cynthia as I grabbed a linen shirt to tie around my waist.

"Since I'm working a double tomorrow, I better take advantage of a little time off tonight. I'm just going to stroll into town and chill out the coffee place," I had said. (Could they hear my voice shaking?) "I think there's an open mic poetry night tonight."

Cynthia looked up from her laptop. "Yes, it starts at eight."

"Okay, well don't wait up."

Doug smiled. "Have fun."

Fun was not a four-letter-word. But it felt like it.

I walked through the brightly lit center of town and then took a turn onto Osbourne Street and started down it. The air was warm and the town was alive with summer people. Just as Luke's direx had said, after I walked about five minutes I came to a small triangular intersection, and to the right was a two-story brick apartment house. I went to the door in the center and pressed the button for apartment four. Within a few seconds the door buzzed unlocked and I pulled its heavy glass frame open. As I ascended the stairs, I heard a door open above me and footsteps sound on the wood flooring. I peered up and saw Luke looking down at me.

"You made it," he said, his smile turning a little bit shy.

"Whose apartment is this?" I asked as I reached him.

He thumbed back at the door. "My bud Ollie's. He just went to get pizza."

I followed Luke into the apartment and said, "You have a friend with a place? Why aren't you crashing here?"

We entered and I saw the standard white walls, wall-to-wall carpeting, and living room that opened into a galley kitchen. Except . . .

Luke looked sheepish. "Well, this is actually his sister's place . . . but she's out tonight."

"Gotcha." That explained the extra-wide teacup with

three floating pink roses in the middle of the coffee table. And the big silver LOVE sculpture that adorned the top of the refrigerator.

Luke shut the door and gave me a hug. Not as bearish as the one by his Land Rover. Sort of baby bearish. "So what's this all about?" He bit his lip nervously.

"Umm...." What *was* this all about?

A broken track record with guys. My relentless heart. Luke's burdening secret. All of the above.

I closed one eye and kind of grimaced. "Umm. I needed to get out of the house and you're the only person I know in Mattamuskee?"

Luke laughed and threw his head back. "Oh. Excellent." He walked into the kitchen and got a beer out of the fridge. "Want one?"

I shook my head.

We sat on the couch and stared at the baseball game on TV. It wasn't the Red Sox and it wasn't very interesting. I wanted to do a big-exhale gum-flap like my dad, but I didn't. Instead I decided to stop being unsure of myself. I was the one in control here. Not him.

"So what's with your hair?" I said. A total nonsequitor.

Luke laughed and ran a hand through it.

"Dude," I continued, my voice sounding like someone else's, "why don't you shave stripes into it anymore?"

He looked at me from the corners of his eyes and smiled. "You liked that, eh?"

I made a face. "You were such a badass back then, what happened?" I poked him in the ribs.

Luke faked an innocent face. "How could an ordinary guy like me be a badass?"

I nodded in disagreement. "Oh yeah. You know it! *Dangerous.*"

He smiled. Then he looked at me stone cold for a

second. "You're right. It's the most ordinary that are the most dangerous, no?"

I caught his eyes. I didn't know what to say. We were just joking around, right? Everything felt awkward.

"Uh . . ."

Luke put his arm around me. "So what's with *your* hair, April?" he said. "Why don't you ever let it down?"

I touched the bun on top of my head and thought, *I think that's what I'm trying to do right now.*

Right about the time when I thought for sure Luke was going to lean in and kiss me—no lead up or anything, just my being there on the couch next to him seemed like reason enough—the apartment door burst open and a big guy carrying pizzas and a six pack came in.

"Yo," he said, giving me and Luke a chin nod as he went to the kitchen.

"Ollie, April. April, Ollie," Luke said as the guy put the pizza down on the counter.

"What's going on, April?" Ollie called from the other room. I heard the fridge open and close. I could see the back of him from a mirror in the living room. He was wearing baggy shorts and an oversize rugby on his tall frame.

"Oh, nothing," I said, putting my hands in my lap and shrugging my shoulders at the mirror.

He turned and our eyes met in the mirror for a second. He winked and took a bottle opener to the beer.

Then in walked three more guys, like a parade from frat Mattawhiskey, all in cargo shorts and rugbies, all carrying their own designer six-pack, with hair lengths ranging from sporty short to hippie long. They marched into the narrow kitchen and filled the fridge. When all the guys spread out in the living room on chairs and floor spots, the pizza boxes made it to the coffee table and slices were distributed. I sat in the middle of the couch in between Luke and some random guy and squeezed my knees together.

Was it just me or were they all staring at me when a commercial came on?

It was just the sound of the game on TV, the occasional grunt or comment about a player, and then the chewing chewing chewing of greasy pizza going down. There were five guys in one cramped apartment and me. What was I doing there?

I got up to get a glass of water and a paper towel for my hands. When I opened a cabinet, I saw that Ollie's sister had a nice selection of glasses, different-colored blown glass, and glasses in funky shapes. I wished she was here so I wasn't all alone with the lacrosse club. Did she even know they were lounging all over her furniture without even using paper towels for their pizza? I shuddered and tried to shake off my mini-Cynthia-moment. I reached into the cabinet and chose a red-striped glass that got narrower in the middle, almost like an hourglass. As I was filling it up with the pitcher from the fridge, Luke came up to me.

"Hey," he said softly.

I tried to give Luke a normal smile, but all I could think was, *Yeah, hey, it's me, Idiot Girl, so desperate to see you that I crash boys' night. Want some water in a pretty glass?*

No wonder it was so quiet in there—it wasn't from eating; the guys couldn't be themselves with me around.

"Hey," Luke said again, coming closer and whispering in my ear, "let's eat and then get out of here, okay?"

I rolled my eyes. Oh my God, he sensed it, too. "No, no, no," I said, pushing him gently away so he could look at me and see how serious I was. "I'll go." I shook my head and motioned to the guys. "I totally didn't mean to barge in. I don't know what I was thinking."

I knew what I had been thinking.

Guilt. I constantly replayed Hunter's near-accident.

Longing. I wanted to talk about it some more with Luke. Reassess my nanny skills with something other than the nanny manual. Have him look into my eyes and tell me it wasn't my fault. That everything happens for a reason. That the reason was . . .

And maybe some other kind of longing. I hadn't told Doug and Cynthia about Luke's presence—not because I was doing Luke a favor, or because lying was no big deal to me.

But because I liked him.

Cue the long overdue sigh.

As I stood there in the kitchen staring at dried red roses hanging next to the light switch, I admitted it to myself again: I liked him. And maybe I had liked him for all those summers before. Maybe that Like with a capital L had never really gone away.

But now I was trying to hide behind a cool hand-blown glass while he was having guys' night in. And I was blowing any chance I ever had with him. Easily. Steadily. Day by day.

Luke looked at me like I was crazy. "No, I'll just get another slice and then we go for a walk or something." He made it sound that simple.

I put my finished water on the counter next to the sink and smiled sweetly. "*No-nah-no,*" I said, accidentally slipping in to my Hunter-mode. "I'll see you tomorrow, all right?" I headed for the door.

Luke put his arm in front of the doorway to stop me from moving past him. He spoke intently. "But I want to see you tonight."

"Umm. Are you trying to be bossy-scary or bossy-sweet?" I said. I kind of laughed.

"Sweet," he said, giving me a point-blank stare. Then he rolled his eyes.

"Okay," I said, tossing up my hands in surrender and being all dramatic, like he had finally talked me into it. "One slice and we'll go."

I told myself that there was nothing bossy-scary about Luke as we walked Crescent Beach near the Rogers' home.

Except there was. For one, he was a guy. And two, I was a girl. And, he was a guy that seemed to know exactly what to say to a girl. And, I was a girl that seemed to not know what to say at all.

But as he reached for my hand, and then as we held hands walking down the beach, I decided I wasn't going to be that girl anymore. Steph was right with all her lectures back at home. I could say—and should say—whatever I wanted. And people—guys—would want to hear it. Should want to hear it. So I did.

"So what are you afraid of?" I said. "Like, what's your biggest fear?"

Luke pretended to pierce his own heart. "Ouch. First you attack my hair, now you're putting me in therapy."

"You're afraid of therapy?" I teased. I had never been around someone who made me want to know absolutely everything about them. I wanted to know all of his important memories, what he thought about small things, big things, what he'd been through, what he wanted to do. I was gripped with an intensity to know him.

All of him.

"I am very afraid of therapy," he said, smiling. "Having

had two years of it, I can tell you, I am afraid of going back."

Was he joking? What had he gone into therapy for? Now I was worried. Maybe I should have started with an easier question, like, What's your favorite food? I wanted to know that one, too.

"What's your favorite food?" I said, bending down to pick up a stone and throw it into the waves.

Luke stretched his neck to the side. "Sausage."

Eww. Okay, so far this wasn't exactly working.

"Umm, what's the worst thing you've ever done?" I said. Oh shoot, that was probably just as bad as the fear question. I wished I had consulted a deck of dating cards so I could have thrown out some more appropriate questions.

Luke stopped and took my other hand in his. He faced me and swung my arms in a mirror image with his. "What's the worst thing I've ever done? What is this, some kind of twenty-questions' game?"

I nodded and said, "Mm-hmm."

He craned his neck way back and sighed. "Okay, okay. I don't know. Lying? Cheating? Stealing? Which one?"

I laughed. "What, you've never killed anyone?"

He laughed back. "Not that I know of!"

"I guess cheating, then. That's pretty low."

Luke gave me a sly smile and we kept walking. "Well it was sixth grade and it was the hardest math test of the year. I only copied the bonus question, though."

I swung his arm with mine. "Oh, sure." I could do this. I could flirt. I could let my hair down. I could run naked into the ocean with him right then if I wanted to.

Or . . . not.

"So, what about you?" Luke squeezed my waist. "What are you afraid of?"

This moment. His closeness.

I looked at him. "Nothing. Not anymore."

Luke pulled me in and gave me a soap-opera Romeo face.

"I don't want to kiss you here," I said before he could get any closer.

He laughed. "Oh yeah? Why not?"

He was getting closer anyway.

I sat down. "Because you're a dork. And. You haven't even asked me what *my* favorite food is," I said.

He sat down next to me and guessed, "Calamari."

I shook my head.

"I think *you're* the dork." He guessed again. "Salad."

"Nope." I tried to keep him guessing but Luke just drew in closer to me.

"What's your favorite food, April?" he said into my ear, his breath hot and his teeth gently nipping at my earlobe.

"Mmm,"—total schoolgirl melt—"okay, I'll tell you. It's vegetarian sushi rolls."

"Nice," he said, kissing my neck and torturing me by not kissing me on the mouth. I could do this. I could totally do this. This wasn't like any of the other times with guys back home. This felt way intense. And real. And straight out of some two-star, girl-meets-guy movie that I would never admit to liking. But even saucier than the movie version—this was happening to me.

No lie.

"Umm, Luke," I said, taking his chin with my hand and turning it toward my mouth.

He pulled back and gave me a taste of my own medicine. "Not so fast, you have to tell me what's the worst thing you've ever done." He pushed himself back in the sand and propped himself up on his elbows. He sat waiting for me to answer, enjoying the game.

What did Luke say? Lying, cheating, stealing? What would I say?

Letting Hunter lie to his parents. Lying to myself that it was okay.

Cheating Steph out of a friend who took normal, healthy risks—non-life-threatening risks—and being someone who was always too afraid to say what she meant. Cheating myself out of me.

Stealing away to Mattamuskee to make my last summer before college count. Stealing a part of Luke's heart? Stealing my own back.

"What's the worst thing I've ever done?" I said, trying to make the next part sound natural and not rehearsed. "Not kiss you."

And then, in a matter of seconds, that answer disappeared, just like the wave in front of us as it rolled to shore and then receded. Luke sat up and kissed me once—one tidal wave of my heart and my brain colliding with my libido—and then I leaned in and kissed *him*. I closed my eyes to the sound of another small wave trickling in to shore and then retreating. And we sat there a while, just kissing, and I knew I would never regret that moment.

Not then.

FOUR WEEKS BEFORE THE ACCIDENT

After that night at Crescent Beach, everything started happening really fast.

The morning came with gleeful shouts from Hunter as he realized that the circled red day on the calendar had finally arrived. He went around shouting that Luke was taking him to WaterWorld. Just him and *not* Rosy, and that they were going to go on all the water slides, and the splash park, and ride the mechanical waves. Doug and Cynthia had already left for work when Hunter embarked on his WaterWorld announcement, but I was glad for the heads up.

I went down to the basement to find Luke asleep on the old plaid couch and I woke him up with a kiss to the forehead. He smiled like I was a sweet alarm clock, and I wished he could stay in the basement just a few more days. Or until the end of my time there.

Cynthia and Doug went straight to Boston after work, and, as Hunter and I watched a special movie after dinner, I tried to imagine the words Luke was using to break the news about his failed internship. I knew he would probably be MIA for a while, but part of me was relieved I wouldn't have him around to obsess over. At least not until next summer maybe.

Hunter had been asleep for an hour or two when I heard the garage doors clank open in a steady rhythm. But when I went to the kitchen window to watch the Rogers pull their car in, I was shocked to see Luke's Land Rover, in all its safari glory with no windshield, pull up behind the silver Volvo sedan. And Doug was driving it while Luke rode shotgun. Cynthia pulled the Volvo into the garage and Doug parked the Rover in the driveway. I watched as they all made their way into the house. I started filling up the teapot to give me something to do.

Doug unlocked the door and they greeted me warmly.

"Everything went off without a hitch," I said, smiling and faking a yawn.

Cynthia slipped her heels off and held them in her hands. "April, I have to run to the shower, but Doug will explain everything." She pointed her eyes in Luke's direction and headed for the stairs.

Luke went into the bathroom immediately, shutting the door loudly.

"How was your speech?" I asked before Cynthia was out of the room.

She turned to me and smiled. "Fabulous. Thank you." Then she looked at her hands holding the shoes as if they were dirty and went upstairs.

I put the teapot on the stove as Doug came toward me. In a hushed voice, he said, "Luke wasn't in any condition to, ah, drive," he said, spiking his eyebrows up. "His, uh, internship lost its funding. Or rather, the science lab's federal funding was reduced, so his position was cut."

"Oh," I said, squeezing my legs from behind the counter.

Doug continued to defend Luke. "You can understand he'd be upset. He had a few too many at Cynthia's function. Didn't make a heel of himself or anything. Just wasn't in the right frame of mind to get behind the wheel, if you know what I mean."

Drunk driving? Yeah, I'd heard of it.

Doug was rubbing his hands like the night had been too long for everyone. "That being said, with the funding cut, so was his stipend and housing. He's, uh, been trying to get something else going before he came to us."

"Oh, sure," I said, turning around and reaching for the boxes of tea. Lying lemon or cheating chai?

Doug's voice was apologetic. "I know my son. I could tell he was keeping something from us. We eventually got it out of him. He wanted to sort everything out on his own. A real go-getter, just like his old man."

"Oh," I said again. "Okay. Understandable." They'd bought that story of his?

Doug smiled so I smiled back at him. Luke came out of the bathroom and stumbled toward us. Doug turned to him. Luke was standing in the foyer doorway, holding himself up with one arm.

"You remember April?" Doug said to his son.

Luke looked at me with the goofiest of masks. "I do."

I waved from the kitchen.

Doug turned to me. "I've just got to duck upstairs for a minute. I'll be right back." He glanced at the teapot on the stove. "Perhaps you could make that black?"

I nodded. I watched Doug go up the stairs and I wasn't sure what to say to Luke. But I didn't have to worry about it for too long. Luke hurried up to me and blew a big, intentional breath into my face. It reeked of beer.

"Lovely," I said, backing up.

He laughed. "I'm not drunk!" he whispered.

"Huh?" This was getting weird.

"I drank five non-alcoholic beers tonight!"

I checked the stairs to see if Doug was coming back yet. "Umm, why?"

Luke knocked my forehead like it was made of wood. "So I could come back here, silly. To see you!"

I bit my lip. "You had to pretend to be drunk to come back here?"

Luke was acting sort of drunk, actually. "Uh, duh"—he looked over his shoulder—"if I hadn't, then Cynthia would have shipped me off to my mom's."

"That's weird," I said. "Why didn't you just actually get drunk?" I asked.

"Who knows what would have happened then?!" he said, like some crazed insane asylum escapee.

"Okay, good point." I guess. . .

"And now I've got the weekend to convince my dad that I should stay for the rest of the summer." Luke folded his arms across his chest and looked proud.

I felt a little cheated, but I wasn't sure why. The teapot started whistling. I could hear footsteps on the second floor. "Are you kidding me?" I said, stealing a knowing look at him.

He shook his head and laughed.

"I thought I got rid of you last night," I teased. My heart was jumping around.

Luke just shook his head again.

THREE WEEKS BEFORE THE ACCIDENT

Friday's e-mail came like kismet for Luke. I tried to pretend it didn't matter either way to me. The e-mail wasn't from a fully funded science lab offering Luke a new internship or anything like that. It was a reply from a whitewater kayaking trip out west. Someone had canceled the same day that Luke had e-mailed his résumé for the advanced training. I guess he had written so passionately about realizing how he wanted to live his life—hurtling down a river in a plastic boat—and about his kayak experience back east, that he got the slot. They were actually sponsoring him with the promise that he would train other kayakers at one of their branches on the east coast. Luke was beaming like never before. No one could wipe that smirk off his face.

We spent all day Saturday and Sunday staring at each other, saying anything. All things random, unimportant, and steeped with hidden meaning. How are you? Hanging in there. Me, too.

We spent the weekend staring out the window as it rained on the ocean, turning it into a hazy grey-blue blur. Waiting to see if Cynthia would ship Luke off to his mom's condo in northern New Jersey. I wondered if he could read my mind.

Sunday night, Luke was given full house privileges for one week before he flew out to Colorado.

Doug and Cynthia had agreed to let him crash in, well, his bedroom, right next to Hunter's. I guess in their pushing-forty- and fifty-something minds, leaving the two of us alone in the same house for a week was not long enough for things to develop into something real. Especially during daylight hours with kids around. But I knew that the week would stretch on forever, and that we would take advantage of every spare minute. And that when night came, just because they were in the next room, it would not stop us from seeing each other.

TWO WEEKS BEFORE THE ACCIDENT

Monday

We met secretly in town, at night, desperate to see each other even though we had just seen each other all day, taking care of the kids at home. Luke held my hand as we walked in the middle of a quiet street, up a hill, the smell of the sea salt air near. He put his hands around my waist and drew me in. I tilted my neck to look up at him and he kissed me there in the middle of the street. I think someone with a dog walked by on the sidewalk. We didn't care.

Tuesday

He picked me up at the coffeehouse in town as it was closing at ten o'clock. In his Land Rover, a blindfold was resting on my seat. It was one of Cynthia's silk scarves, and Luke tied it around my eyes. He drove through the summer night, the warm air whipping through our hair, as I waited in the blackness to discover where we were going.

"When are you going to get that windshield thing fixed?" I teased. "I think I just ate a bug."

"Here, it was just a black fly," he said, wiping my mouth with the back of his hand while he drove.

"A true gentleman," I said.

Luke was driving a zigzag maze of lefts and rights. Inclines and declines. Crazy turns that I was trying to visualize with the blindfold on.

My stomach did the work for me.

When we stopped, he kissed my hand, then held it as he helped me out of the car. Luke walked behind me, his two hands on my hips, as I walked forward with the blindfold still on. He kissed the back of my neck while we walked. He turned me around and kissed me with the blindfold on. He kissed me as I untied it and looked around and saw we were at Mattamuskee Bluff, the stars an enormous canvas overhead, the moon our own personal nightlight. He kissed me and whispered he loved me.

Luke's fingers were everywhere. His hands felt warm. My body felt warm. He was touching me like the crazy turns of his Rover. My skin felt tingly, dizzy, like my head was still in the blindfold. He brought us over to a couple of random trees in the middle of the deserted parking lot. He started to unbutton my shorts. I stopped him and said, "Not here."

Wednesday

While Hunter was digging a moat in the mud around his island, and Rosy was propped up in her sun chair watching the ocean roll in, I lied down on my stomach in the mud and looked at Luke. He was sitting up, near to me, his legs forming a diamond in the mud. The tide tickled my toes as it gradually eased closer to our spot on the beach. I inched myself closer to him, so my right arm rested casually in the diamond of his legs. I started slow, tracing my finger up his calf and to the edge of his long board shorts. Then I let it sneak up his shorts and touch the inside of his thigh. I just kept tracing a line up and down his inner thigh, as if I were drawing the reeds of a bow, as if I were writing a story about my feelings for him, as if I were making a map to tell him where my heart was. Luke crept his fingers on my shoulder, like a spider crawling, and did a tickling little dance down my arm.

Thursday

Luke and Hunter were doing an afternoon bike ride, making loops around the block. They were going to pass by the house so I was sitting in the grass with Rosy in my lap, waiting. Hunter came first, his training wheels wobbling under him as he navigated. Luke followed behind on a mountain bike. As he passed by in a three-second whoosh, he looked at me and mouthed the words, "I love you!"

ONE WEEK BEFORE THE ACCIDENT

I knew he was coming that night, after everyone fell asleep. That's why I was propped up on my bed, reading a book in the pale glow of a reading light attached to the bed's headboard, and wearing my black Calvin Klein bra, black boy-shorts underwear, and black knee socks. I was lying flat on my back with my legs up on three pillows, holding the book, when he came in.

"You rock," he said.

I laughed and turned to him. "I'm not a chair," I said.

He didn't think it was that funny.

"A rocking chair?" I said.

"Yeah," Luke said, sitting down next to me and stroking my leg. "I got it."

Luke smiled and took the book out of my hand and threw it on the floor.

"Hey!" I said. "Noise factor?"

He looked at my copy of *Crime and Punishment* and said, "Carpeting." Then he said, "Why are you reading that?"

I bit my lip. "Because bad things happen. I want to be prepared."

"Not with me," he said, attacking my neck like a vamp.

Luke got on top of me and my pillow mountain was squashed as he took me in a bear hug slash world wrestling championship stronghold.

"What are you doing?" I whispered, laughing.

"I want to take you with me, to Colorado." He nuzzled my neck.

"Ha," I said. "You couldn't pay me to get into one of those death traps."

He took no offense. He just said, "So what *can* I pay you to do?"

I tapped his back. "Don't be gross."

Luke pulled away and gave me a look. It was the one I had grown used to. His eyes were totally infused with attention. Every time he looked at me like that, it was like he never wanted to look anywhere else. It was the first time I had really seen that kind of affection from a guy's eyes. Pointed at me.

"I could stare at you forever," Luke said.

I looked away. "Okay, you can take off your cheeseball aftershave," I said. But I actually liked it when he said things like that.

"Done," he said, and stripped off his shirt.

I pressed myself closer and let him run his fingers through my hair, felt his hand move along my shoulder and down my arm. I tilted my head up to really study him, to imprint his expression on my brain, to see if he was for real or not. Those seconds when he held me, before he kissed me, stretched on and on. The moon shone in through the window and landed all around us in white light.

Then he pulled his face back and looked at me. There was a question in his eyes but it already had the answer in it.

"You cool?" he said, and his voice came out kind of shy.

I nodded. "Uh-huh."

Luke only looked at me for another second before he closed his eyes and moved his lips toward mine. When he kissed me, I closed my eyes and kissed him back. Every time we kissed, it was like that first time at Crescent Beach. I had never been kissed like that before. Tender and determined at the same time. Even though his mouth was on mine, and his two hands held my back softly, it felt as if he was touching and kissing every part of me. Like his kiss was saying a lot more than just kissing.

I was ready for it. It felt like I was going insane. A kiss like that needed to last and last. And it did. For a long time. We pressed closer and closer. He ran his finger along my side and felt the curve where my waist met my hip bone. He started feeling under my bra, and I pulled a sheet up over us as he pulled up my bra and began undoing his shorts while he kissed my ribs.

"You smell so good," he said. Now the cheesy comments were starting to sound a little fake. Either that or I was dead nervous.

"Johnson's Baby Shampoo," I said.

Luke laughed. Then he pointed at his hair. "My dad's shampoo for grey hair. Oh yeah, I'm working it." As he said this he took off his shorts and put them on the floor. I took off my bra while lying under the sheet and we went back to making out.

All the stuff that should probably take two people a really long time to work up to, we were doing in a matter of minutes.

Luke's hands were everywhere so I tried to do the same but I just couldn't get the image of Doug's Silver-Shine-for-Men shampoo out of my head.

Luke was getting really heated up and pretty soon the piles of clothes on the floor were complete.

"Did you bring a raincoat?" I said as he started to get on top of me.

"Huh?" Luke looked down at me.

"I mean, a *condom*," I said.

"Oh, right." Luke bit his lip. "Uh, no."

I wrapped the bed sheet around myself and walked over to the dresser. I pulled a green glow-in-the-dark condom out of the top drawer and waved it at Luke. He was just lying there on the bed like some Greek god. Not at all embarrassed. I shuffled back to the bed and tried to lie down without appearing like a human mummy.

I handed him the condom and he unwrapped it. He held it under the reading light for a few seconds and then he flicked out the light. I released the sheet from around me and slid over to him as he put the condom on.

"Cool," Luke said, "I'm like a human flashlight."

"Not for long," I said, shocked at my own bravado.

Oh god.

"Whoah," he said, like he was in way over his head. He got back under the sheet and started kissing my mouth and then pushing his little flashlight into me. "I can't believe you have these funky condoms," he whispered. "What else do you have up your sleeve?"

I smiled and just rolled my eyes. "My mom's an OB like Cynthia. Well, you know that. She's had me carrying condoms since I was thirteen," I said, realizing as the words came out that I was drifting farther and farther away from the moment.

Luke was just listening, sort of.

"Don't worry, you're not going to pop my cherry or anything," I said, sounding way more experienced than I was. I laughed. "But I'm also not carrying them around because I have a disease or anything, so don't worry about that."

Oh geez. Way too much talking.

Luke was too busy grinding his hips into mine to respond. No, I wasn't a virgin, but sex was still a foreign country to me, but Luke seemed to know what he was doing. Where he was going.

I let him grunt quietly and cover my neck with his hot breath. I let him go on and on and on. I couldn't stop thinking. About random stuff. Prom. My mom's office with free condoms. Steph coming to visit. Rosy just across the hall.

After a while he was pushing so hard inside me I thought that something might break. Like my body. But then he finished with a muffled groan and laid his entire weight on top of me. I couldn't breathe. I pushed up and he got off of me, pulling the condom off as he did.

He set it on top of the wrapper and we reached for each other. I pulled the sheet over us.

"The glow's over," he said, looking at the condom.

"No glow," I said, not sure what else to say.

There we were, lying in a tangle of tan lines, with our clothing in two little lumps on the floor. After a minute, I reached for my boy-shorts underwear and started putting them on. Luke stood up, buck naked, and flicked on the bedside reading light.

Oh my God, I just had sex with a Greek god glowing under the dim light. I swear the moonlight was shining on him, too.

Luke bent down and cracked open a beer he had brought. Then the Greek God stood in front of the window, downed half his beer in one gulp, and let out a belch.

"Are you kidding me?" I said.

"What?" he said, pulling on his shorts and coming to sit next to me. "This is me. This is who I am. Don't you like me?"

I eyed the condom off to the side and wrinkled my nose. "Apparently, I do."

Luke held my chin in his fingers and kissed me again. "I'm just nervous about Colorado, you know? Leaving after meeting you and all."

I let out a big mental *aww*.

"No lie?" I said, ignoring the aluminum can in his hand.

"I'm going to miss you," he said, and his eyes gave me that love look. No one had ever missed me before. I wondered how long he would miss me for. Long enough to come find me again?

The night was crisp and quiet, except for the dim hum of the air conditioner. Luke was smiling like it was his job, and I was replaying the past few minutes in my head.

I didn't know what else to say, but in that moment it felt like my whole entire summer had shifted. That something that had begun when he walked in the Rogers' sliding glass door had morphed into something entirely new. Things were weird and bittersweet all at the same time. I looked up at Luke and smiled.

"You should go," I said. "No lie."

But Luke took my hand instead and pulled me back down on the bed for an embrace.

As if it were the most normal thing in the world.

As if we were a new boyfriend and girlfriend getting to know each other. Gazing at each other, holding hands and feeling each finger over and over again, rubbing each other's wrists and palms and kissing each other's fingertips.

My bedroom was quiet and peaceful and as we lay there, things felt right.

For a moment.

He whispered one thing before sneaking out of my room.

"You'll come out with us, right? For one last hurrah."

THREE DAYS AFTER THE ACCIDENT

The two-by-three-inch card in my fingers was lime green with a string of petals framing the information. Rather flowery for a lawyer's business card. I held it in between my pointer finger and thumb and read the name in lavender: Diane Williams, attorney at law. Her address and contact numbers followed. I closed Doug's rolodex and slipped it into my wallet.

Just in case.

Doug and Cynthia went back to work. So did I. Together, we had come up with a short list of duties for my first day back on the nanny manual bandwagon.

    1 low-structure, free play with the kids
    2 explain the D word to Hunter
    3 laundry
    4 pick Luke up from the hospital

Hunter and Rosy and I were sitting in the muddy sand at low tide, letting it tickle our toes as the ocean slowly receded. Rosy was learning to sit up all by herself now. Hunter thought it was funny that we could form a little wall of wet sand around her backside to help support her. Occasionally she would get excited by something—a seagull coming close or a child running by fast—and her whole body would sway in excitement, then topple over to the side. Hunter thought it was hysterical that his sister was getting covered in sand.

"Can we bury her?" he asked, a look of hope in his eyes.

"No," I said, "but you can put mud on her toes. She's the baby mud monster." I dripped bits of mud over her arms. Rosy had fistfuls of sand and was putting it in her mouth, then spitting it out, forming a muddy trail down her chin. She was smiling and cooing. Hunter was jumping around like a jester, doing silly things to entertain her. Being with them was like breathing again.

Hunter got to work digging a hole and building up the walls so we could fill it with water. I extracted some mud from Rosy's mouth and dipped her hands in a bucket of water. It was pointless. A second later she had refilled her hands and mouth with mud. Hunter was back and forth to the ocean, filling up buckets and then dumping them in the hole.

Doug and Cynthia had promised to come home early, so we could connect as a family. I was going to finish my job in Mattamuskee before I headed home to get ready for school. But I wanted to add a few things to our low-structured, free play list:

5 pretend none of this happened
6 skip the funeral
7 start over

Hunter didn't fully grasp the accident. That was where "explain the D word to Hunter" came in. I wasn't sure which one to start with. Dying. Death. Dead. Drunk. Deceit. Disgrace. I took a deep breath and interrupted his imaginative play. A crew of rowdy pirates was attacking the island he had built.

"Hunter," I said, scooping sand out of Rosy's mouth.

"Yeah?" His shoulders were beach-tan and his hair had turned a shade lighter since summer began.

"I wanted to talk to you about something."

"Okay." He kept playing, not looking at me.

"Have you been wondering why everybody's been angry and crying lately?"

He nodded into the pirate pool. "Yeah."

Only a child would stand by and watch the drama without asking what happened. He might have thought his mom and dad were planning a trip away. Without him. Or maybe he thought that we were crying because of something he did. Like the time I got mad and mini-yelled at him for decorating the windowsills with CDs. He knew he wasn't supposed to touch those, let alone take them out of their cases and prop them up in the sunlight. So what? They did shine pretty nicely. I shouldn't have gotten so upset.

"Well," I continued. "Luke and I were in a car accident on Saturday night. Did you know that?"

He shook his head. "Did the car go on fire?" he asked.

"No," I said, "but it hit a big rock and got pretty smashed up."

A few seconds later he said, "Why?" He was listening, but he was still busy looking at the sand and the water and lining up pebbles around the edge.

"Well," I started, my mind going back to the accident and trying to figure out a way to explain it to him. "The car was going too fast, and Luke tried to slow it down, but –" I caught my breath. Oh god. I had just slipped. I stopped and bit my lip, then started over. "Umm. What I was trying to say was that Luke was in the car, too, and he got hurt, but he's okay. He's in the hospital. He'll be home this afternoon."

Hunter looked up. "What happened to him?"

I pulled Rosy onto my lap and dunked her hands in the pirate pool. "He hurt his arm and part of his leg. He's not going to be able to go swimming or to the playground for a while. We're going to have to be extra nice to him when he comes home." That or ruin his life by telling him that he was the one driving.

Hunter nodded.

Then I said, "You know Luke's friend Ollie?"

Hunter said "Yeah" and spiked a rock into the pool of water.

"Everybody was crying because he *died*." There it was. The D word in all its glory.

Hunter didn't say anything for a while. So I continued, "Luke is going to be sad, and that's okay. It's okay to be sad. If you're sad, just let me know." Hunter wasn't close to Ollie, but I knew it would be difficult for him to see Luke physically hurt and grieving at the same time.

"What's died?" Hunter asked.

I squeezed Rosy into a hug and breathed out. Wow. This totally felt like a parents' job.

"Have you ever seen a worm on the sidewalk that can't wiggle around anymore?"

Hunter perked up. "You mean like when you cut it in half and then it makes two worms wiggling around!?"

Okay, bad example.

"No, not really, umm –"

Then Hunter broke in. "Oh, you mean, like, died, when Grouches the Bad Bunny stopped hopping around and my friends Lily and Lisbeth were looking everywhere but he had hopped away to live with another family?"

I had no idea what he was talking about. What were these people teaching their children? "Tell me about Grouches the Bad Bunny," I said.

Hunter knelt in front of me and started talking fast like he was explaining the meaning of life and only had ten seconds to do it. "Okay, okay, so Grouches was this bunny. And he lived out in the *hatch* in the back. And, and, Lily and Lisbeth said it was their pet. But their mom said no it wasn't because it was on the other side of the *fence*. But they said, no, no, Mr. Walker let them *pet* it all the time. When Grouches got bigger Lily was going to keep it under her bed in her room."

I listened, nodding, giving him the stage. He was nodding as if his life depended on it.

"And, and, one day Grouches wasn't there. And Lily's mom said he hopped away to live with another family. But Lily's dad said he died and was going to be food for Mr. Walker's big snake." Hunter looked at me, pleased, like he had just solved a mystery.

"Yes, Hunter, yes. It's kind of like that. So do you understand what it means when something dies?" I could feel the knot in my throat working its way up. I remembered Ollie.

He shook his head at full attention. "No."

"Okay. So When Grouches the Bunny died, his heart stopped beating, right?" I put my hand on Hunter's chest. "This is your heart, right?"

He nodded.

I continued, "So when a bunny's heart stops beating, it can't hop anymore, and it just lies there still. That's what it means to be dead."

Hunter absorbed this. He went back to digging with the shovel. Rosy reached for her sippy cup that was coated in sand granules. I sighed out and said, "So if Luke acts sad and wants to be alone. Or if he seems angry. He's not mad at you. He's sad that his friend can't get up and play with him anymore."

Hunter didn't say anything more. Okay. I had done my duty. I thought that death would be a huge, major deal to Hunter. Totally mind-warping and heavy. But he seemed to act as if it was just another fact of life. Sandcastles crumble, sippy cups leak, friends die.

Hunter was busy digging in the sand, so I said, "I'm going to take Rosy out to the water and try to wash her off a bit."

He jumped up to come and we walked out to the ocean. Hunter ran, of course, skipping ahead in the sunlight. I looked at his small frame and wished I could freeze him at that age. I wished I could prevent him from being the friend or the driver in a Land Rover in fifteen years. I wanted to teach him how to learn from past mistakes, but I didn't know how. I was still making my own.

FOUR DAYS AFTER THE ACCIDENT

The afternoon Luke was released from the hospital, he was waiting for me in a wheelchair with a nurse standing behind him. When the kids and I picked him up curbside, I tried to ignore the deep guilt within, knowing Ollie was not among the patients being treated and released. So I focused on picking up Luke's prescriptions with Rosy on one hip and Hunter begging for Charleston Chews at the register. I kept myself busy setting up his air mattress in the playroom so he didn't have to crutch it upstairs. (There were so many toys that could roll underfoot, I wasn't sure if this was any safer.) Charging up his cell phone. Fixing us all a snack. Even coming to his rescue when he said he couldn't get his fly zipped up.

I knelt before him in the bathroom and worked on the stuck zipper. "Did you do this on purpose?" I asked.

Luke laughed. First time I had heard that in days. "Wish I had been that clever," he said.

I got the zipper up and stood to face him. It was a rare

peaceful moment. Rosy was sitting in her exersaucer chewing on a toy and Hunter was building a tower of supersized Legos up against the refrigerator. I cocked my head at Luke and said, "Are you all right?"

He breathed into my hair and said, "Yeah."

It wasn't very convincing.

I hugged him and pecked his cheek.

I closed the bathroom door so we could see out but Hunter couldn't see in. "Can we talk about the accident?" I asked. Every household duty in the world couldn't keep it off my mind.

Luke leaned closer and kissed my neck.

"No," he whispered. "Not now."

I wanted to tell him that he was driving. That it could still be our secret. But that he had to know. For his own sake. And mine. I couldn't manage knowing this and being the only one.

"Why not?" I said.

And then we were kissing and he had his good arm snaking around my side and his hand was plunging into the back of my shorts.

I pulled back for a second and, laughing, said, "Didn't you just get out of the hospital?" I wanted to laugh, but I wasn't there yet. Not even close.

He nodded even though it was a rhetorical question. "I missed you so much," he said. Feeling his muscular chest and one strong thigh rubbing against mine made me shiver. Kissing his warm mouth and nuzzling his hair made me melt. I wasn't about to give in though.

"You need a bath," I said, focusing on the smell of antiseptic around his arm.

"Yes . . ." His eyes lit up.

That's not what I meant.

"I need to talk about the accident," I said, trying to

ground him.

Luke ignored me and kept kissing my neck and touching my chest with his one good arm. I peeked through the crack in the door. The phone was ringing, but the kids were fine.

"Seriously, I do," I said. But it really felt good to be making out again. It helped wash away all the anxieties of the police stuff.

"We will," he said, chewing on my earlobe, "can you come visit me in the playroom tonight after everyone goes to bed?"

"To talk?"

He nodded innocently. "Mm-hmm."

"No," I said. I ran my hands through his hair and kissed his cheeks. "I know what you're trying to do and it's not working."

"April!" I heard Hunter's voice on the other side of the door. I spun around to see him peeking through the crack. "It's MOMMY!" He was holding the cordless phone up to his ear. "Yes, Mommy. I found April. She's in the bathroom with Luke." Hunter handed me the phone. "Here you go!"

I opened my mouth wide at Luke and he shrugged. Hunter ran back to his Legos.

"Hello?" I said, hoping that no one was on the other end of the phone and Hunter was just playing pretend. He did eat invisible fruit, after all.

But Cynthia's voice came across loud and clear. "April! I was just checking in to make sure Luke made it home from the hospital okay. What's the matter? Did he fall in the bathroom?"

I stood there staring in the bathroom mirror as I spoke to her. "No, no one fell down." I waited for a reply. She was quiet. I continued, "So, uh, yeah, I got him from the hospital and we got his meds, and —"

She cut me off. "Hold on."

I gave Luke a look through the mirror and mouthed "Help." He was still practically on top of me, so he could hear every word she said. He grabbed my boob. Jesus. What was wrong with him?

Cynthia got back on the phone. "Sorry. I was just checking my pager. One of my patients is 10 centimeters dilated. Look, we'll talk about this later, okay? You know the funeral is at 11 a.m. tomorrow, right?"

She hung up.

How could I forget?

FIVE DAYS AFTER THE ACCIDENT

Cynthia and I were on kid duty at the back of the church while Doug and Luke sat up front and absorbed the funeral in full intensity. There were four hundred people there, crammed into and spilling out of Mattamuske's little Methodist church. Lots of young people crying their eyes out. Tons of family. The girl I had seen at the hospital, Ollie's sister—I had held her water glass in her apartment under the LOVE sculpture—and the guy on the bike, his brother, up in the front row with their parents and grandparents.

I kept taking Hunter outside for breaks. He couldn't sit still and Rosy was happy in Cynthia's arms, like she could snuggle there all day. I hated listening to Ollie's friends speak about his generosity, his humor, his wild passion to take on the world in travel. He had been so many places, done so many things. He had so much more to him than I had seen that one night. Being there in that church, and knowing I had a place in the ending of his life's story was brutal.

I didn't want to hear another song played, or catch another Boston Red Sox reference, or listen to the minister speak of heaven and Ollie living on in our hearts. I didn't even know him, but I was wrapped up in the final moments of his life. I wasn't supposed to be there. Right? But I was holding on to a piece of the puzzle that nobody knew was missing. I took lots of deep breaths outside with Hunter as we listened for bird songs, and he searched the sky to spot one in flight.

"There are no birds out today, April," he said. "Where have all the birds gone?"

"I don't know; I really don't. Maybe they're all sleeping."

Hunter shook his head. "They must be taking Ollie up to heaven." He stared up at the clear sky and nodded. "They'll be back."

I stared at him in amazement. I took him in my arms and hugged him, told him he was right. "Do you know how smart you are?" I said.

He shook his head.

"You're so smart because you think with your brain but also your heart." I put my hand on his chest and felt him breathing.

"Huh?" he said.

I smiled. "You're a good boy."

He was satisfied with that.

"Listen to my heart," he said.

I put my ear up to his size 4T white button-up and

listened. For a moment I flashbacked to doing the same on Ollie's bloodied body. I pushed the memory away.

"Tha-thump, tha-thump," I said.

Hunter smiled. "I'm alive!"

"You are."

Hunter looked at me with a little hesitation. "When are you going to die, April?"

I held his hands gently and smiled. "Not until I am really, really, really old. Same as Luke and your mommy and daddy and Rosy. Not until you're all really, really old."

"Are you sure?" he said, nodding quickly.

"Oh, yes, I am sure." I hugged him tight.

I wanted to believe my words, make them come true for him.

I wanted to change what was going on inside the church and take him away from the threat of death.

I wondered at what age he would realize my words were assurances and nothing more.

Hunter took my hand and we walked back into the church. We stood to the side as several guys carried the casket down the center aisle. Luke trailed behind them on his crutches, unable to help carry Ollie's body before it went to the cemetery.

I looked past Luke's grief, his tears, and the devastation he faced.

I needed to hear assurances to my own questions.

Did he really not remember the accident? I wondered if I should I even tell him that he was to blame.

We had been waiting in the reception line for thirty minutes when I saw her. We had just gotten close enough to the door to see into the large hall where Ollie's family stood, greeting every single person as he or she filed in. I saw her embrace Luke and hold his head in between her hands. She was wearing a light pink shirt and grey pants. She was tall, and from her profile I could see she was related to Ollie.

Cynthia and I were next in the family greeting line when Doug appeared out of the hall and took the kids off our hands. She turned to me and offered a face of condolence. "Are you ready?" she asked.

Did I have a choice?

Cynthia introduced herself and shook hands with Ollie's sister. She shook hands with the brother and repeated her phrase, "Cynthia Rogers. I'm Luke's stepmother. I am so sorry." She kept going, leaving me to follow in her footsteps.

The sister reached out her hand.

"I'm April Nichols. I'm Luke's friend. I was in the car when —"

She embraced me. "Oh, God, you poor thing," she said. "I'm Nanette. I am so sorry."

"Oh, no, not me. Please don't —"

The brother reached over extended his hand, "Xavier Baker. Thank you for coming. My parents wanted to meet you." He reached over and alerted his parents to who I was. As I shuffled down the line, the mother took my hands and looked at me with her blotchy, swollen face.

"Will you give us your e-mail?" she said. "We would like to keep in touch. Talk about the accident. Not today." She shook her head. "Today isn't about the accident."

I nodded. "Of course, of course. I am so sorry for all of this."

The father was next to take my hands. His voice was shaking loudly. "I am so sorry, April," he started saying.

I shook my head. No. Don't say sorry to *me*.

He fought to get the words out. "I am. So Sorry.

Oliver. Put you in this. Position. I am so glad that no one else was hurt." He burst out into a big nose blow in his handkerchief.

Oh, God. This was what a nightmare felt like.

"He didn't," I said, "put me in any position. We all made mistakes that night. It wasn't his fault."

The family blew their noses simultaneously and thanked me for my words, for my assurances that I did not blame Ollie for this tragedy. If only they knew how much he was *not* to blame.

I moved on and tried to shake off the difficulty of staring into their eyes and seeing their pain. I walked toward the tables where Luke had gone before. Hunter was in his lap but Luke was fading. I had been at this funeral long enough to die inside and then regain myself.

"Hunter," I said, breaking their bubble. "Wanna go outside?"

Luke turned around in surprise and his eyes searched mine.

"This is too much," I said.

Luke nodded, but he didn't understand.

Hunter didn't want to go outside with me, so I went by myself. I opened my cell phone and hit Steph's number. Relief flooded over me when she answered.

"Oh my God," she gasped. "I can't believe you're calling me from the funeral." She sounded like she had just won a horrible prize. Maybe it was her way of downplaying the shock. "Are you okay?" she asked.

"No, and it just got worse." I started walking away from the church. "Hold on, I'm outside. I just need to get farther away from everything."

Steph waited.

"I met the family."

Steph gasped. "Oh no."

"Yeah. Bad. I keep thinking that I am not supposed to be here. I don't even know these people."

But I was there. Yeah, I was. It's all my brain can focus on. Like some demented film being played over and over.

I continued, "I may have made the wrong choice, or many wrong choices, this summer, but I'm not going to now."

Steph's voice came slowly. "Go on."

My breath caught. "I can't."

She sighed, frustrated.

Then I said, "Hold on."

I watched as Luke walked outside with a bunch of guys. They had taken their suit jackets off but were still wearing ties and white shirts, shuffling around sadly in their leather shoes. Hunter was not with him, and Luke was interacting as naturally as he could. But his body language signaled that something was off. I didn't think it was his injuries. Or even the funeral.

"Hello?" Steph said. "You still there or did you hang up on me?"

I nodded even though she couldn't see me.

I was still there.

Kind of.

Sort of.

I was pretty much frozen in shock at what was going on in my mind.

Luke was in the middle of the bunch of guys outside the church. They were all patting each other on the back at random times. For the first time since the accident, it all came clear to me.

He knew.

~ ~ ~ ~

Cynthia was driving Rosy to napland and Hunter was on his way to a postfuneral playdate. It was an inconsequential thing we were doing, winding through the picturesque side streets of Mattamuskee, but my hands were shaking. I tried to appear calm as I pulled out the cell phone and started tapping out a text message.

"We're going to be sorry to see you go," Cynthia said. "You really stepped it up this year, April, managing Hunter and Rosy together. You're really becoming an important part of the family. In a more authoritative way." She smiled. "You could probably rewrite the nanny manual off the top of your head. We will always be thankful that you had everything under control this summer."

Her words soothed me for a second. Yeah right.

I thought of Hunter keeping the secret. Navigating the steep trail at Mattamuskee Bluff. Almost getting run over by an SUV.

"I'm glad it all worked out. I definitely won't forget this summer," I said with a forced smile, and finished the text. I scrolled through to find Luke's number.

"God, what a day," said Cynthia. "You'd think being a doctor would make this easier, but it doesn't."

"What *does*?"

Truth? Honesty? A clear conscience? Doing the right thing? I thought of the lawyer's business card in my wallet.

Cynthia sighed and turned onto the playdate street. "I don't know. Time. Lots of time. But I don't think anything really erases the tragedy of it. Makes sense out of it."

I thought of Ollie funneling beer at the party, high-fiving his friends, and making the waa-waa sound when Luke pulled the keys out of the Rover.

I heard his words on the road up to the cliffs: *Slow down, man!* And we rounded that last turn. How could Luke not remember any of that?

I reread the text and hit SEND, then waited for a reply. My heart was thumping.

As Cynthia was unbuckling Hunter for his playdate, Luke texted back.

Luke came home before dusk. I didn't look out the window to see who dropped him off. Doug had told us that Luke would be at the Bakers all day but would be home for dinner. I already knew that. While I was prepping dinner, I had texted: Falafel and rice in 45 mins. He had replied: K.

During dinner with Doug and Cynthia, I casually asked Luke if he would like to go down to the beach with me for a walk after dinner.

We had already set this up over the texts, but he said, "Yeah. I need to see the ocean."

"I promise I won't leave you stranded if your crutches get stuck in the sand," I said.

He looked at his dad and Cynthia and said, "Would that be all right with you guys?"

Doug nodded and swallowed his falafel. "No, she should definitely leave you stranded."

Doug snorted. "No, I think it's an excellent idea." We were all trying to act normal, but it felt false.

"The ocean is so revitalizing," Cynthia was saying. "So healing." She was moving her arms around like she was doing a modern dance. "The sound and the smell."

For me it triggered the memory of the crash. The sound of the waves as I sat alone waiting for the ambulances.

Luke looked me in the eye.

Like he was right back there with me. At the accident.

"Yeah," he said. "That sounds great."

"Let's go down here," I said, pointing to a secluded section of the beach that had big black boulders.

"Okay." He put both crutches under one arm and started hopping feebly on one leg.

"Whoah," I said, "are those pain pills still working? 'Cause you're going to need them after this workout."

Luke didn't smile at my joke as he kept going down to the area with the rocks on the edge of the shore. We sat down with our backs against a big rock and I breathed in the salty air. I gave myself a pep talk. Remain calm. Do not cry. Just be honest.

"So what's this all about?" he said, putting his arm around me and kissing my neck. God, it felt good. Maybe the whole talking thing was overrated.

"I just need to talk to you," I said, melting into his shoulder. I kissed him a little to remind myself of all the good things about him. I kissed him to remind him of all the good things *about me*. He might not want to kiss me after tonight.

"What's the matter?" he said, eyes on mine, opening me up.

God, he just buried his best friend. Why was I doing this?

The answer came shooting at me. Because he just killed his best friend. And now he was killing me.

I started slow. "The funeral was hard today." I looked at the water, watched the tide coming in.

"No shit."

Ouch. Knife to the heart.

"I mean, as an outsider . . ." I searched his eyes for truth. "What was it like for you?"

"Sucked." He just sat there like a kid who was being interrogated by his mother.

I cleared my throat. "Okay, about the whole accident thing. It's hard for me to talk about this, because I have feelings for you, right? Like, big feelings." I was motioning with my hands, but I don't think it was helping. I adjusted myself on the rock. "But there's something I need to say."

"April! What the –? Do you realize that we just went to Ollie's *funeral*?" Luke was digging his crutch into the sand and making a hole. "Jesus!"

"Look, look, I am sorry. I know the timing sucks. But I just want you to be honest with me. Just don't lie to me to my face. Now is as good a day as any to talk about something difficult." I gave him a plaintive look, begged him with my eyes.

"Lie to you? What the heck is going on in your neurotic little mind? When have I ever lied to you?"

I bit my lip. His words stung. This side of him was too raw. *This internal anger.* I breathed out. It was just insecurity that was making him say those things. It was just a cop-out because he wasn't being honest with me. With himself.

I put my hand on his crutch. "Luke, listen to me. We need to talk about the accident. Just once. Now. We don't ever have to rehash it again. But I need to talk about it with you."

The breeze on the shore was cooling down. The sun was surfing off to the right, glowing more orange as we stayed on the rock. The sky around it was turning a pinky-purple glow. I took his hand and tried to calm him down. "I'm sorry," I said, kissing his neck. "But I need to ask you something."

"Shoot," he said, still mad.

"Okay. I'm not a walking Breathalyzer test, but you and Ollie and Steph were all drunk, right?"

He tensed his shoulders up. "What, and you weren't?"

"Well, I definitely didn't drink as much as Steph. She was puking and passed out. And you and Ollie are guys, so it's safe to assume you drank more than I did."

He looked defensive. "We have to, we weigh more and metabolize things differently."

Thank you, seventh grade health class. And you held the funnel up to Ollie's lips to speed this process up? I continued, "Okay, I guess I just don't get why you don't remember anything past the kitchen keg with Mike. You just didn't seem *that* drunk."

"April?" Luke said. "Do you want me to feel guilty about going to a party and drinking? Maybe you should Google the word *blackout*. It's called a blackout for a reason."

I wouldn't let his anger get to me. I had to keep going. I listened to the crashing waves to give me strength. The crashing of the 1967 Land Rover echoed in my mind.

"Luke, it just seems really convenient that you don't remember anything, *that you had a blackout*. You don't have to answer any questions from the police. You don't have to answer anything from your friends . . . you don't have to answer anything from *me*."

Luke's body language changed. I could tell he wanted to rip my head off. But he controlled himself. "Ask me whatever you want." He motioned to the beach. "You've stranded me here crippled, ask away!" He shoved his crutches into the sand and made a fist with his one good hand.

"Tell me what you remember of the crash." I spoke slow and steady, not judging.

"I don't remember it!" Luke's face was fierce.

I didn't believe him anymore. My heart sank.

"Let me say some words that might trigger a memory," I said, the thumps of my heart growing stronger. I pictured the swampy side-cut road when Luke tried to steal the steering wheel from Ollie. I imitated Ollie's maniac voice. "Get your hands off, you ninja warrior!" Then I did his British accent. "Oh, you bloody wanker!"

Luke stared at me stone cold.

"Waa, waa. Game over." I made Ollie's robot voice.

"Why are you doing this to me?" Luke said, his voice coming out rough. He swung with his hand and it made his crutches fall out of reach. "God dammit!"

"Do you remember?" I asked. "Can you see it?"

Luke narrowed his eyes. "Yeah, you do a great imitation of my old friend. So why are you torturing me?"

He still wasn't admitting to anything. I looked into his eyes, wishing I could just read his mind and not what he chose to say to me.

"Why were you so angry about him taking the Land Rover?" I asked.

"What?" he seethed.

"Why were you so angry?"

Luke shook his head at me. He stared out at the ocean. "Mother-F'er."

Something was brewing.

I looked at him hard and said, "The anger wasn't just because he took your Land Rover. It was beyond being angry that he jeopardized our safety. And Steph's. Once you had control of the Rover, why didn't you just let it go?"

Luke laughed bitterly. "What are you talking about? Do you want me to relive every emotion I've had since the party? Do you want me to drive off the fucking cliff myself?" Luke tried to stand up, forgetting that he couldn't balance. I jumped up to steady him before he fell down.

"Give me my friggin' crutches," he said. I leaned over and handed one to him.

Luke shoved it under his arm and puffed his cheeks out like a big fish. Exhaled.

"So where are you freakin' going with this?" He wouldn't look at me, but he was talking.

"Luke. I was there. I wasn't drunk. I remember every horrid detail like it has been stapled into my brain. I wake up in the morning: I see your body in that parking lot. I pour a bowl of cereal for Hunter: I see Ollie's brains smashed on that tree. And over and over again I see your hands on the steering wheel."

Luke spit. "You want a medal for all that?"

"No! I want answers! Where were you taking us? What were you trying to prove?"

Luke grinded his teeth together and refused to look at me. The waves crashed harder and closer to us.

I didn't touch him as I said, "Keeping it in won't change it. But telling me might."

Luke angrily threw his crutch in the sand. "Leave me alone!"

I shook my head slowly. "Luke, don't lie to me. You guys switched seats on that side-cut road. *You were driving when we crashed.*"

He looked at me with wide wonder. Said nothing. His body was trembling and I moved back. He was like a bomb about to burst.

I spoke calmly. "You were angry. Beyond anger. You were speeding." I swallowed hard. "I don't know why you were driving up there anyway."

Luke's eyes were blazing. "April Nichols," he spat out, shaking hard. "You've completely lost it. What are you talking about?" He looked at me like I was insane. "I don't know what the *F* you're talking about."

I wouldn't trust him anymore. "Yes, you do."

Luke was adamant. "I was not driving the Land Rover!"

"Yes, you were! I was there. Were you just trying to scare him? Or did your road rage get out of control? But, Luke, just admit to me that you were driving. I can't live with this secret anymore."

"What, are you bugged or something?" He looked over his shoulder toward the beach parking area.

"No, I am not bugged." My eyes widened at him.

He used his good arm to pat me down while he shook.

"Get off me!" I said, jumping back.

"Give me my other crutch!" he said.

"No, Luke! Stop lying to me!" I stood away from him and shivered.

Luke stared at me with hate. "*You* told the police that Ollie was driving. *The entire party* told the police that Ollie was driving. Now you're trying to frame me." He shook his head and let out a loud *"Why?!"*

"Stop twisting everything around!" I said. "I'm not trying to frame you!"

The sun was setting and the beach was growing darker as we yelled at each other. We were totally alone on the shore.

Luke slammed his hand down on the rock. "And now you've decided that you're changing your story and you want me to go to jail? What, is this blackmail? What do you want from me!"

My mind was reeling. "Luke, listen to yourself. This isn't about revenge. Or blackmail!" I stepped closer to him, begged him with my face. Tried to make him see the guilt I was dealing with. "This is about Ollie's family. Knowing the truth. How can you live with yourself?"

"Dammit, April, I wasn't driving the car!"

I stood up and kicked the sand. "Stop lying! You said you have no memory of the accident! A *blackout* from the keg in the kitchen all the way to waking up in the hospital. If you expect me to believe you, Luke, then why aren't you amazed at what I am saying? Falling apart at the news? You're just sitting here defending yourself against something you said you don't *even have any memory of*! How can you be so sure when you claim to remember nothing? I remember everything and it's killing me!" My voice echoed against the ocean and I screamed out in frustration.

Luke scrambled for his other crutch and fell forward in the sand. He broke down crying. I didn't go to him. He was elbows down in the sand, wailing like some wounded animal. After a minute he pushed himself up to sitting with his good arm and leg. He wiped his nose on his bare arm and looked at me, face red and streaked with tears and sand. He was filled with disgust.

"No one is going to believe you, April," he said. He held my gaze. "Not Doug. Not Cynthia. Not even the police. Why would you change your story now? Unless you were going to get something out of it." But Luke, trembling in the sand beside that rock as the waves crashed in, had eyes of fear. He could tell me a million times that what I said was a lie, but he knew it was the truth.

I shoved his crutches at him and walked away.

For the first time, I didn't look back.

I ran up the wooden stairs on the outside of the Rogers' house and sat on my third-floor balcony and cried.

I watched as Luke's dark silhouette lay in the sand for a long time, then my eyes followed him as he started to hobble up the beach on his crutches, slow and methodical, like every ounce of his soul ached. He would stop and wipe his face, then dig his crutches back in the sand and keep moving.

When he got to the road he sat down on a bench made of driftwood and pulled out his cell phone to punch in a text. I reached into my pocket and made sure my phone was on. But as I watched him there on the side of the beach road, my phone did not jingle or ring.

He wasn't texting me.

I washed my face quickly and headed downstairs. My timing was perfect. Cynthia and Doug were busy putting the kids to bed so I scrawled a quick note and took the keys to Cynthia's Volvo. I knew I looked awful.

I pulled up to the driftwood bench and lowered the passenger-side window.

"Get in," I said.

Luke stared at me with eyes of ice.

"I've got a ride coming," he said.

"Get in or I'm calling the police right now."

He sat there and punched a message into his phone like he was being sentenced to forty years to life. He raised his eyes at me and hoisted himself up. Then he opened up the door and got into the car, resting his crutches between his legs.

I pulled the car out and just started driving. I didn't have music on—there was only the chill of the air conditioner as we winded our way down the coastal road that passed Crescent Beach. I didn't say anything, just waited for him to talk. Five minutes down the coast and nearing the border of another town, he still hadn't said anything.

When I spoke my voice sounded more confident than I'd ever heard it. I wasn't coming from a place of fear anymore, I was coming from a place of truth. "Look, tell me where the after-funeral gathering is and I'll take you there."

Luke stared straight ahead. "Are you kidnapping me?"

How could he joke at a time like this?

I shook my head. "No. But you're going to tell me what happened before the night is over."

"Is that right?" His voice challenged me.

"Which way?" I said, stopping the car by the side of the coast. I stared out at the ocean and its endless infinity as Luke told me which way to go. I looked at him once before I turned the car around. How could someone I had felt so connected to seem like such a stranger?

The Accident

~ ~ ~ ~

Luke gave me directions as I drove. Before we would approach an intersection, he would anticipate it and say right or left. Sometimes we would approach a stop and he would just tilt his head forward to signal going straight. For the first ten minutes, it felt like we were going in circles, cruising through all the neighborhoods of Mattamuskee. After a few more minutes, Luke pointed to a fork in the road.

"Take that one and it will lead you out to the highway; go north."

"Go north?" I said.

He nodded. "Just for five minutes. That way we avoid more of that in-town traffic."

The more we drove the farther away from our conversation I felt.

I got on the highway and followed the red taillights ahead of me for several minutes. Cars passed me on the left and I breathed out. Soon this all would be past us.

"Next exit," Luke said, adjusting the crutches.

I pulled off and noticed Hunter's and Rosy's car seats in the back. I thought of their smooth little faces and their searching eyes. Their brains were always on autoscan, or something, to detect other people's intentions. I glanced at Luke, still sandy from the spill on the beach, and wondered why I had gone so crazy for him. Maybe I was just in love with the idea of being in love. Maybe the idea of him falling in love with me was too hard to ignore.

"Take a right," he said, pointing. "See that duck pond? Turn there."

I did, and the car turned onto a narrow road. I followed it for a minute until we reached a dead end. There was a large square-shaped gazebo overlooking another small pond. The area was dark and just the faint glow of the moon behind thin clouds provided light.

"I think we took a wrong turn," I said, coming to a stop in front of the gazebo. I didn't start turning the car around. I just stared straight ahead. Waiting.

Luke didn't say anything for a second. "Nope, I think this is good."

My stomach began tightening. "We're not going to the after-funeral thing?"

Luke was quick with his response. "Nope."

The darkness of the dead-end road surrounded me. What had I done?

I wanted to talk. But not here.

Okay, think think think, April. Turn the car around and drive to a public parking lot or go home.

Luke snatched the keys out of the ignition and held them tightly in his fist.

"God!" I said. "What's wrong with you?"

He fisted the keys. "What's wrong with me? What's wrong with you?" He threw the keys at me and they hit me in the shoulder and bounced down.

"Aah!" I said, grabbing the keys. I fumbled to put them in the ignition and couldn't. I was shaking so hard my fingers wouldn't work. My vision was getting blurry.

I couldn't breathe.

I suddenly felt like I was going to throw up. I pushed open the car door and fell outside. I slid Cynthia's key chain into my pocket as I walked to the gazebo, my breathing becoming fast and labored.

The headlights lit my way the short distance to it. I entered the gazebo and leaned against the low railing. I cupped my hands over my nose and tried to slow down my hyperventilating. I looked at the swampy pond and saw lily pads floating on the surface. Things started to come back into focus.

The headlights switched off and I heard a car door shut. Luke's crutches made little noise as he made his way toward me. He stood several feet away from me, his leg in a brace elevated off the ground and his other leg planted on the ground. He stared at me for a moment before leaning on the crutches to come over.

"April," he said, shaking his head and speaking in a soft voice. His eyes were glossy and he wiped them with the back of his hand. He looked broken.

He didn't say anything so I went to him. I reached my hand out and touched his. This was someone that I really did love. Whatever love meant. But as I held his hand there in the dark of the night, I knew I had to let him go.

I leaned toward him and kissed him on the mouth. I smelled his hair and his neck and let him kiss my neck. I didn't want to do this. I didn't want to do this. I didn't want to do this.

"April, I messed up," he choked out. He fell apart crying. Then he let out a mournful cry, *"It was an accident!"* His voice echoed over the duck pond.

Relief washed over me. He knew what had happened. He had admitted it.

I pulled him close to me in a hug and the crutches went crashing to the ground. I started crying, too, like there was an actual string to pull that turned me from a put-together person to a blubbering mess in an instant. The lily pads on the pond and the shadowy moonlight came in and out of my vision as Luke and I clung to each other. Luke pulled back and we lowered ourselves to sitting on the floor of the gazebo.

Something changed in his face. "But you saved me, April, you saved me."

I shook my head. No. No. No.

"When I woke up at the hospital and saw your face. Like an angel in my dreams. And Dad said that Ollie was driving. I knew then and there that a divine force was working for me." He was holding my hands and looking at me pleadingly. "This was why we met. This was why you came to Mattamuskee. To save me. From myself."

I inched back and leaned against the short wall. "No, I didn't." I shook my head vehemently. "It was a mistake." I remembered the way Colonel Morris had phrased things when he reconstructed the crash. It was almost as if he had tricked me into saying Ollie was driving.

It was true, at the time of the crash, the driver's seat was waaay back, just like when Ollie was behind the wheel. So that was evidence, right? All bases were covered. But in that moment when Colonel Morris had questioned me, had I subconsciously wanted to erase Luke's murder? So much that I had lied without really thinking?

But then I lied about the same question again.

And again.

I couldn't tell that lie one more time.

"Luke, I lied to the police. *You* lied to the police. It doesn't matter how or why anymore—it just matters that we set it straight."

"*Ollie's dead,*" Luke seethed. "Me going to jail is not going to change that."

The sick feeling in my stomach returned. He was kind of right. But I couldn't give in to him. I didn't want to hurt him, but I had to be strong. For myself. For Ollie's parents. They deserved to know the truth. I owed it to myself to do the right thing.

"April, this will all just go away. I promise. This is so fresh right now. But we'll regret it, I swear we will. I love you. I wouldn't ask you to do this if I didn't love you."

"What? You're asking me to lie for you," I said. If he truly loved me, he wouldn't ask me to carry this weight. "Don't you get that?"

"You don't want to see my life destroyed, too, do you?" Luke was pleading me with his eyes.

"But it's not right," I said.

Luke reached down and clutched my hands. "None of it is right, I know! The whole thing is a disaster. Ollie's *gone*. I can't even believe that *that* is true. But bringing me down with him isn't going to bring him back."

"I don't want to bring you down," I said, repeating his words, my arms starting to shake again, "but Ollie's family deserves to know the truth. I don't think I can go on keeping this secret!" I covered my face with my hands and breathed in the warm air of my breath. "How can you?" I wheezed out.

"It wasn't intentional," Luke spat out, regaining some of his wrath from the beach. "I didn't do it on purpose!"

I was trembling even as he wrapped his arms around me. I spoke quietly to him. "Luke, *what* happened?"

He gripped my shoulders tighter and let out a low groan. "Argh, it's ridiculous. God!" He hit the ground with his fist. "My anger. It. Was. So. Pointless."

I breathed evenly now and faced him. I waited.

Luke spit on the ground. "He screwed my chances at that science lab, all right! I just had some pent-up aggression toward him for being part of why I lost that internship. Not that I even wanted it. Not that it even mattered."

My mouth hung open. "God."

"What?" he said, anger rising. "Isn't that what you wanted to hear?"

I shook my head. It wasn't what I was expecting or wanting. And it still didn't explain the night to me.

The crash.

I knew no other way to say it.

"Luke, look at me."

He lifted his eyes to meet mine. "What? I was mad."

My voice was in a hush, disbelieving. "And you killed him for that?"

Luke's eyes rolled back in his head. He started to shake like a stick of dynamite about to burst.

"You don't understand! He was being an a-hole that night and I was going to dump his sorry ass at the cliffs and make him camp there overnight!"

It all kept flooding out. "But I lost control of the Rover. It was an *accident!*" he cried out to me. To himself. To Ollie. To Ollie's family who couldn't hear him.

"I didn't mean to! I was just going to drop him off!" Luke was sobbing and wheezing and crying out painfully in the dark night. "Just have him camp out under the stars." Everything he had been holding in since the accident came out. "He'd do the same thing to me. It's what dudes do." Luke was a mess.

I looked at him with a mixture of relief and confusion. "I don't know what to do," I said.

"Don't do it, April," he sobbed. "It's not worth it." Luke was begging for his life. He trembled as he held my face in hands and repeated, "Don't do it . . . don't do it, don't do it."

I whispered low and quiet into his shoulder, so quiet I didn't know if he could even hear it. "I'm sorry. I'm so sorry." I held on to him as tight as I could and tried not to let go.

ONE WEEK AFTER THE ACCIDENT

I woke up at six a.m. in the lavender sheets up on the third floor with its ocean view. The sun was coming in and casting a soft light to the room. The blinds were up, and I hoisted myself up on my elbows and looked at the water. There it was, as vast and deep as always. I lay back in the bed and pulled the sheet up. I twisted my head on the pillow, trying to loosen up my neck. I had no idea how I was going to do this.

I closed my eyes and thought of random times this summer. I thought of nights spent studying the nanny manual until one night Luke tossed it aside and wrestled me, tickling my ribs until I cried. Hunter handing me his sandwich crusts after a meal. I thought of standing on the edge of that cliff and throwing a rock down the jagged edge before we left the peace sign rock. Making a wish. I wished I could go back and freeze things when they were simpler. I just wanted to go back to Crescent Beach and never leave. I wanted to go back to the days of lying on the beach on a

Tuesday morning with children too little to know better. I wanted to go back to feeling innocent and in love and like nothing could go wrong with the world. I wanted to go back to hearing Luke tell me he loved me megaphone-style on the lawn at the party. And I wanted to stop there. I didn't want to leave the party. I didn't want to have the rest of the night haunting me every single second of the day. I didn't want to wake up every morning and see Ollie's blood forming a puddle, a river, an ocean of sadness in that parking lot.

But I couldn't go back.

Life was about moving forward.

And that was something I had to do.

I pulled the cell phone off the nightstand and dialed Steph's number.

Steph's cell phone rang and rang and then went to voicemail. I hung up and dialed her number again. It rang several times and then I heard her pick up.

"I don't remember asking for a wake-up call," she said, her voice sounding sarcastic and asleep.

"I'm so glad you picked up," I said. The clock read 6:06 a.m.

Steph coughed. "I'm so glad you called. This couldn't have waited three hours?"

"Are you alone?" I asked.

Steph was waking up. "Uh yeah."

"Steph, listen to me. He was driving the Land Rover."

"What are you talking about?"

I took a deep breath. "*Luke.* He was the one driving the night of the accident. Not Ollie."

I waited for her response.

Dead silence.

The seconds ticked by.

I looked around my room. The sun was growing

stronger. Seashells I had collected were on the windowsill, bearing silent witness.

Steph spoke softly. "What? I don't understand."

"Listen. You have to swear to me that you will not utter a single word to anyone about this. I am going to take care of it. I haven't talked to a lawyer yet, but I will. It's just that I have to protect myself, you know? I mean, I have a few more days left here. I have the kids' safety to think of, my own, Luke's."

"Luke's?" she spat out. "Sorry, but, what the—why are you worried about his safety?"

I scratched my head and thought about the car ride home from the gazebo the night before. After Luke's big cryfest in my lap, we sort of pulled ourselves together and hugged for a long time. He told me he loved me. I told him I knew that. He said he wanted to start fresh. In a final pang of anger, he threw his cell phone into the pond and we watched it hit a lily pad and then sink underwater. Luke didn't want to go to the funeral after-party so we drove home slowly. He spent a lot of time rubbing my knee, crying quietly, and thanking me for saving him. Pretty much messing with my head in a major way.

"I'm worried about Luke's safety because, a) he just lost his best friend, and, b) I just told him last night that he was the one driving. That he killed his friend."

"Oh my God, April, what?" Steph gasped. "You mean, you knew? And *he* didn't know? I'm confused."

I couldn't lie to my best friend. Was avoiding the question the same as lying? "Umm," I started. "He's said from beginning that he had no memory of the crash."

"But everyone at the party saw Ollie driving." Steph's voice was suspicious.

"Look. It's complicated, okay. I'll explain it all to you when I get home. I just wanted to tell you"—my voice hushed to a whisper—"that Luke was driving. Okay? So you know. In case anything happens to me."

Steph was wide awake now. "What? What could happen to you?"

I tried my best to sound calm but the tears of fear and loss and exhaustion were coming to the surface. "Nothing's going to happen to me. I mean, I could get run over by a bus tomorrow, you know? That's all I mean. I am going to finish my job here. I have to do everything really carefully, okay? Can you respect that?"

Steph's voice was comforting. "April, are you in some sort of trouble? Do you want me to come back out there and get you?"

"No, I'm not in any trouble." But Luke was. "Just let me do this my way, okay?" I said.

Steph agreed. "Now I am never going to fall back asleep," she said.

I heard Rosy's morning coo come across the baby monitor, and I hung up with Steph.

When I walked into Rosy's room, it was dark with little slivers of light framing the edges of her room-darkening shades. I pulled the shade open and stood in front of her crib. Rosy was lying on her back, sweaty-faced and kicking. I picked her and up and nuzzled her face into my neck. She still smelled like last night's baby soap. I cradled her in my arms and looked at her innocent, smooth face. She looked up at me with big, open eyes, waiting for something more.

I touched her flat little nose and pressed gently. "You promise me that you'll never get into any trouble, okay?" I said. Rosy blinked and smiled as if to say she understood.

Hunter was running around the beach like a maniac. It was late afternoon and his shoulders were a freckled brown. Rosy was sitting up and kicking her feet in the muddy sand. Eating more sand. We had run out of swim diapers so her regular type was bulging out of her baby bathing suit, expanding as water seeped in from the ocean.

The kids and I had spent our last days doing extra-special fun things. We went to a children's museum, a zoo, and ate ice cream after nearly every meal. Luke stayed at home, a self-imposed prison. Whenever we would see each other in passing, his eyes were begging mine to tell him what I was going to do. I reassured him over and over that I wasn't going to tell. That I was just going to leave and say good-bye to it all.

I didn't know if he believed me. Part of me wished I *could* just leave it all behind me.

"Hunter, come here, I've gotta tell you something." He

raised his arms like airplane wings and came in for a crash landing. On my lap. I kissed the top of his head. "I've had so much fun with you," I said. "You definitely made my summer."

"Made it what?" he asked, cupping a handful of mud and covering my knee with it.

"Made it worthwhile," I said, noticing a cargo ship off in the distance.

"What's worthwhile?"

I squeezed him, knowing this would be one of the last times we had together. "Worthwhile means that I had so much fun with you, I learned so much from you, that you made my summer really great."

I was filled with relief. Knowing I had a plan. Knowing I would be leaving soon. I was also filled with dread that I wouldn't see Luke anymore. But I was so mad at him. He deserved everything he would get. I shook with the weight of it all. Soon it would be lifted.

Hunter smiled through his little teeth and tilted his head up at me.

"You learned lots of stuff from me?" he asked.

I nodded, lighting my eyes up to a yes.

"Like how to boogie board?"

I laughed. "Yes, you definitely taught me that one."

"And you learned how to read from me?" he said.

"Oh yeah, sure, that too."

His confidence was inflating by the second.

"And shoot a gun, and draw a pirate ship?"

I nodded. "You got it."

And I learned to be more honest with myself, to ask more questions, to cry for no reason, to cry for lots of reasons, to keep trying to be better, to not be afraid to jump in waters too deep. There had to be a lesson in everything. That's what I learned from being with Hunter every day.

Nothing was inconsequential.

"What did I learn from *you*?" he asked, scrunching up his nose.

I shrugged my shoulders. "I don't know. Why don't you tell me?"

He leaned back in the sand and stared at the ocean upside down. The temptation to tickle his belly was hard to resist. But I couldn't disturb how relaxed he was. He just lay there in my lap, stretching backward with his tummy exposed, watching the waves roll in upside down. Hunter spoke matter-of-factly.

"I learned to be good," he said.

"You were always good," I said. We all were at one time. Sometimes we just got lost along the way.

"Yeah." He lifted his head up and snapped out of the trance. "Do you want to see something really cool?" He jumped up and started doing karate tricks.

"Cool," I said. "Hey, can you find me a shell to bring back home? I'll put it on my dresser and that way every time"—Hunter went running off before I finished talking—"I look at it I will think of you." When he came back he was holding a shiny black mussel shell. He handed it to me and looked at me with those four-year-old eyes.

"I am going to send you a bird feather from my hometown, okay? I don't know when I'll be able come back to visit."

I knew turning Luke in would have major consequences. What if Luke denied it and his lawyer fought me? What if I had to go to court? What if I got in trouble for lying in the first place?

I ran my hands along the sand and pulled Rosy into my lap.

None of that mattered.

I was moving on.

"Diane Williams, please?" I said into the cell phone. "Yes, I can hold."

Here I was, sitting on the wooden flooring of the Rogers' back porch, the attorney's business card now folded around the edges from my fingers bending it. My back was up against the sliding glass door. Hunter was engrossed in a cartoon. Rosy was sitting in her exersaucer, glancing up at the TV in between chews on her plastic flower. I turned away from the kids as I waited for the lawyer to come on the line.

A chipper male receptionist put me on hold and then an even more chipper, but raspy-voiced woman came on the line. The conversation started to bleed together like the night of the accident. *My name is April Nichols. I am a nanny for Doug and Cynthia Rogers.* Suddenly, I realized I was talking on the same cell phone I used to call 9-1-1, and my body started to float away. I was hovering over the tigerlily grasses in the backyard. I was floating up above the ocean. I was falling away from what I was doing.

Yes, April, I could hear her voice saying, as if it were coming from a long tunnel. *What can I do for you?*

My words came out fast and unprepared. *I think I made a mistake. I gave the police the wrong information. I'm scared. I don't know what to do.*

Her voice was professional but understanding. I could hear her speaking, but everything was blending together. *You filed a false report? Is that right? I'm glad you called me and not the police. Listen, I am going to help you.*

I began to focus again, to return to my body. But she was still talking, taking me away.

This would most likely be considered a misdemeanor, but it could be considered a felony. The prosecuting attorneys will take action against you. You do understand that?

I turned to look at Hunter and Rosy, to remove myself from what was happening. Felony? Action against me? No. I didn't understand what it meant.

Diane Williams' voice brought me back. *When can you come in to talk?*

"Where's Luke?" I said, looking across the dining room and up the stairs. His place at the dinner table was empty. I had gone to see Diane Williams that afternoon under the guise of "a long walk to clear my head." But I was afraid Luke had gotten suspicious, or worse, had followed me and seen which law office I had entered. Now he was MIA.

"He'll be back any minute now," Cynthia said. "A friend picked him up."

I focused on the white containers of Chinese takeout on the table. I had to forget about him. Cynthia reached across the table and touched my hand. "I spoke to your mom today. They're anxious to see you again."

I smiled. I sensed that my parents were proud of me for sticking it out and for being strong. If only they knew how strong I actually had been through all of it.

Doug gave me a warm smile as he spooned some fried rice onto his plate. "We hate to see you go. But you're always welcome to come back during school breaks. To work *or* to visit."

I wondered how welcome I would be after they found out I was going to crucify their son. To tell or not to tell, that was the question.

Cynthia raised her glass. "April, to you." She clinked her glass to Doug's and they toasted me with toothy smiles.

I took a bite of lemon chicken and shook my doubts away. Of course I had to tell. The lawyer, the police. Luke's parents. Luke was responsible for his own actions. Not me.

I gulped down my water and looked at Doug and Cynthia. They were staring at me like they were waiting for a happy-ending response. I wiped my mouth on my napkin and addressed them. "You have a wonderful family," I started, looking at Rosy, who was sucking on a plastic device with a mesh bag that allowed mashed-up banana to be squeezed out of. "Rosy is so sweet . . . and aware of everything around her. More than I ever knew she would be." By aware, I meant that I could tell Rosy all my secrets, let her watch all my mistakes play out before us, and she'd never betray me. Nor understand how someone who loved her and took care of her could lie.

Doug and Cynthia relaxed in their seats.

I continued, "Hunter is amazing. He's so intelligent, so funny—and what a vocabulary! We had tons of fun." Minus the Hunter-almost-dying moment and minus how he harbored his stepbrother by lying to his parents.

I started to choke up.

Internally.

Because I was still doing it. I was lying to their faces. But I couldn't stop now. I just had to make it one more night until I left. Then the truth would come out. I would rather face them after they had processed the news.

"I have learned so much this summer, and not just on

the kid front, but –" I was interrupted by the phone ringing.

"Let the machine get it," Doug said, waving his hand.

"Okay," I said, pausing for a moment. I took another bite of food and tried to think of what to say next. The answering machine picked up, and Cynthia's sunny voice could be heard saying, "Leave a message!" Just as I was about to go back to my speech, a girl's screaming voice rang out on the answering machine. Cynthia sprang from her chair and lunged for the phone. She picked up the cordless and quickly said hello.

Cynthia's face broke out into panic mode as she listened to a screeching girl on the line. We could hear the cries from across the room. Doug got up and stood next to Cynthia, searching her eyes for information.

"Calm down," Cynthia was saying. "Where are you?"

The girl screeched something back.

"Hang up and call the police!" Cynthia said. "We're on our way!"

She hung up and turned to us with distress. She glanced at Hunter. "Doug, help me get everybody in the car." She wasn't telling us anything because Hunter was there. Doug hoisted Hunter on his back and I picked Rosy up. In a strange kind of daze, we left all the food on the table and immediately followed Cynthia out the door.

Cynthia got behind the wheel and didn't even wait for me to finish buckling the kids in before she peeled out of the driveway. "They're just going to the Marksons," she said, and sure enough, a minute later we were dropping them off at the front door of their confused neighbor, Marcy Markson.

"No time!" Cynthia yelled from the driver's seat. I got back in the Volvo, between the two car seats in the back, and buckled myself in.

As Doug shut the passenger side door he looked at Cynthia and barked, "What the hell is going on?"

Cynthia bit her lip as she sped down the street. "That was the girl Luke is with. They're having some sort of problem."

"Problem?" Doug spat. "What kind of problem?"

"I don't know!" Cynthia screamed out. She was totally hysterical.

"What did she say!?" Doug said. "Why are you panicking?"

Cynthia concentrated on the road. "Doug," she started. "They're at Mattamuskee Bluff. She said he's sitting on the edge of the cliff and he's been drinking."

"Good Lord," Doug said, trying to digest the information.

Cynthia looked over her shoulder. "April," she said. "Luke is asking for *you*."

I took the cell phone out of my pocket and tapped 9-1-1.

"I'd like to report an emergency," I said.

"You have your phone on you?" Doug said, whisking his head around in a daze. He said it like he was relieved, as if he was too stunned to formulate normal, logical thoughts.

I ignored him and spoke into the phone. "My name is April Nichols," I said. "We need police at Mattamuskee Bluff. We got a call that Luke Rogers is sitting on the cliff and he's having a problem." I felt like I was in some weird reenactment where every second counted. It wasn't actually that far off.

The dispatcher started asking me for more information. Doug reached back and snatched the phone away from me. "Dispatch the police, NOW!" he ordered.

The 9-1-1 operator said something.

"Dispatch the police to Mattamuskee Bluff *now!*" Doug ordered. "We'll hold!"

I watched him as he waited. He was somewhat calm when the dispatcher came back. "Thank you," he said.

Cynthia climbed up Cliff Drive and my stomach lurched. I closed my eyes and tried not to remember climbing this hill with Luke. Doug handed the phone to Cynthia and she answered questions. I just stared out at the dark night, put my forehead on the window glass, and closed my eyes.

When we got to the parking lot, I saw a teal sedan parked by the cliff. In the headlights of the Volvo we could see a girl pacing around. Cynthia parked the car off to the side and we jumped out. We went running over to her. The moon was high and full, lighting up the night. Cynthia embraced her. The girl's face was streaked with tears.

"What's he doing?" Cynthia asked, her voice catching as she saw Luke sitting next to his crutches by the edge of the cliffs.

The girl collapsed and pointed at him. She was crying too hard to speak.

"Luke!" I yelled out in his direction. "It's me!" We were about fifty feet away from him.

I saw a bottle rise out of his hands. He tipped his head back, taking a slug. He was sitting on the very edge, unsteady on a rocky outcropping. I remembered those heights, the steepness of the jagged edge below. I didn't have to go any closer to know that the slightest move could send him tumbling down the rock face.

I looked at the girl.

"What happened?" I shrieked. "What did he say?"

She was crying uncontrollably. Cynthia shook her a little.

"It's about Ollie," she sputtered out.

Doug shouted out, "Luke, it's Dad. Don't move. I'm coming to get you."

Luke's voice was scratchy. "April," he said loudly, pointing a crutch at me. "Only Benedict April."

Everyone looked at me. I channeled my inner strength: I was not afraid of this. I walked closer and when I was just about twenty feet away, I took a deep breath and called out, "Luke, I'm leaving tomorrow. Don't say good-bye to me like this."

"Come closer," he said, waving me over with the bottle. "Tell them where you went today. What you did."

"Make me," I countered.

Luke threw the bottle down the cliff. A few seconds later we heard it hit a rock and shatter with a crunch. Crash. The sound of the waves echoed against the rocks. Crash. The impact of the Rover echoed in my soul.

Luke's body was moving slowly side to side. I started to walk slowly toward him. Doug and Cynthia tried to hold me back with their words, but everything was fading away. The girl's cries were being muffled. The noise of the waves hitting the rocks was a dull thump of a heartbeat. The tree Ollie died under shriveled behind me as I walked to the edge. All I could see was Luke. I locked him in my sight.

I stood a few feet away from him, a safe distance from the edge, but close enough to feel my heart start to quicken. Close enough to lock him with my eyes but not close enough to grab him. Or let him grab me. Everything else disappeared. The moon felt like a spotlight.

"What are you doing?" I said.

It wasn't accusatory.

He snorted. "What are you doing, trying to save my life now after you threw it away?"

My words came out easily. "I did it for myself. Not you. I couldn't lie to myself anymore." I let my eyes drill into his like circular hypnosis spirals. Come to me, Luke, come off of there.

"Ha," he said. "So you admit it."

I nodded. "Yeah, now you need to, too."

He bit his lip. "'Zat right?"

"Luke," I said, extending my hand. "What's the worst thing you've ever done?"

He smiled and his eyes rolled back in his head. He lost his balance for a moment. I heard Doug and Cynthia gasp from behind us. The girl let out a wail.

"Luke," I repeated, "what's the worst thing you've ever done?"

He shook his head at me slowly. "*You* know the answer to that," he said, looking at me with the familiar venom. His eyes moved over to the tree where Ollie died, the spot in front of the boulder where the Land Rover crashed. I took another step closer and was so close I could whisper into his ear.

"It's not *that*," I said. I could smell his soapy scent mixed with liquor. I touched his hair and the bottom of his earlobe. I forced myself to not look down the cliff. "*It's not that*, Luke," I said. We were face-to-face now and I could feel his hot breath.

He put his hand on me. "April, don't."

I could feel his strength overpowering me. I couldn't move. We could both lose our balance. Or one of us.

"It's not the accident, Luke," I whispered.

"I *love* you," he said, and it came out pained. I wasn't sure what suffered me more from moment to moment: Ollie's death, my guilt, this fallacy of love. I wanted to believe that he had loved me in some real way, but here on the cliffs again it felt like a game. He squeezed my elbow and I could feel him leaning to the edge.

I took a step back while he held onto my elbow. He had brought me here and I had gone willingly. I was now ready to leave. I pulled away from him and he let go. He balanced himself on his crutch and watched me as I walked backward, locking eyes with him. I mouthed "I love you, too."

There was this insane part of me that did.

I backed up until I was a safe distance again. I looked over my shoulder and saw Doug, Cynthia, and the girl huddled together.

"Luke, I'm coming to get you!" Doug said, breaking free and striding toward his son. Cynthia wailed out "No!" afraid they would both be lost to her.

"Dad, freeze!" Luke said, throwing his crutch over the cliff. It bounced silently out of view. "I'm not kidding. I don't want you up here. I only want April!"

Doug backed away and held his hands up.

"What do you want April to do!?" Doug yelled.

Luke grinned at me and shouted, "Tell them!"

"Luke, stop it," I yelled. "Don't make *me* do this!"

But he just stared at us all and laughed.

I threw my hands up in the air and held them there. "Do you know what the worst thing I've ever done in my life has been, Luke?" I screamed. "Doubting myself. Not believing in myself. Fearing the truth. Sound familiar? But I don't do that anymore. And it's not because of you. It's not because of this horrible accident. It's because I finally know what it means to be responsible for my actions. And I am taking responsibility for what I've done. I'm not going to make that mistake again! So talk to me. Running from this won't be the worst thing you've ever done. Lying about it will!" I was holding my ribs with my arms crossed over me, and my whole body was shaking under the moonlight. He just stared at me like I was crazy.

But I knew I wasn't.

"Come on! Come back!" I yelled.

We stood there staring at each other, waiting for the next play. But I was done. I was *so, so* done. I breathed in the salty air and shivered under the cool night wind. The end of summer was tangible in the air. I could taste the end of my journey on my lips. Misdemeanor, felony, what have you, I was ready for it.

The police cruisers wailed up Cliff Drive and soon they were pulling into the parking lot with controlled speed. The cops shined their headlights on us and came to an abrupt halt. They spoke through a loudspeaker.

"Come away from the edge with your hands up," a cop instructed. I raised my hands above my head and walked to the police cruiser.

"Put your hands up!" another cop ordered Luke.

"He's got a crutch, he can only get one hand up," Doug yelled over. "He's not armed!"

I didn't turn around to see what Luke was doing. It didn't matter. The only thing that mattered was me. And I knew where I was going. No lie.

When I got to the car, a female police officer had me place my hands on the hood as she patted me down. I took a deep breath and craned my neck to take a peek at Luke. He was hobbling down from the rocky outcropping on one crutch with his free hand extended in the air. He was squinting in the glare of the police headlights as they kept their guns trained on him. Then I heard the words ring out through the night.

"It was me," Luke said, loud enough for everyone to hear his moanful cry. "I was the one driving."

The Accident

I breathed a sigh of relief.

It was finally over.

I waited by the cruiser while everyone was questioned separately and Luke was put in the back of the police car.

The female cop came over to me after a while and said, "You're free to go."

For now.

30 MINUTES BEFORE I SAID GOOD-BYE

I had to walk Mattamuskee Bluff one last time.
When the sun started rising, lighting the ocean up into a field of diamonds out my bedroom window, I pulled on a pair of running pants and went downstairs to find Cynthia's car keys. I wrote a note on the white board and locked the front door behind me. I needed to say goodbye to every corner of town, every curve in the road that winded up Cliff Drive. I drove slow, so slow it felt like it was like a totally different road. I examined the grassy growth along the side of the road as the car clung to the right. I concentrated on the bumps in the pavement, the gradual and not-so-gradual inclines. I saw trees I had never noticed before. Little trails made by animals. And then I saw the parking lot looming ahead.

To any other person it looked just like a dirt parking lot at the top of a cliff. But to me it held the scariest moment of my life. It held a flurry of activity that had now all disappeared. This dirt held the blood of a young man's life. I cut the engine and inhaled deeply. I could feel the emotions rise in me like a tsunami.

I locked the car and walked toward the trees. In the distance, I saw that a small cross made of palm fronds was staked into the ground. There were bouquets of flowers. Ocean rocks. A Red Sox hat. I didn't remember seeing this stuff the night Luke confessed, but I had a feeling it had been there. I didn't want to kneel down in the same spot I had been in the night Ollie died. So I stood there, not too close, as I reached into my pocket. I pulled out a little piece of paper and a pack of matches. The paper was folded up into a tiny square so I unfolded it and read the words I had written. It said *I'm sorry*.

The wind that morning wasn't strong, but it was gusting enough that it made lighting a match difficult. I tried three before I put the paper under my foot and kneeled down to create a shield from the wind. The match took and stayed lit, so I cupped my hands around it and brought it to the paper. The paper caught fire, and I took it out from under my shoe and watched it burn.

I walked slowly over to Ollie's shrine while the paper curled up in flame. *I'm sorry* slowly disappeared. First the *I'm,* then the *sorry*. I watched it go letter by letter. I caught the ashes in my other hand as the paper burned up. I stood in front of the flowers. I couldn't bear to look down so I just looked up at the gauzy white clouds as I opened my hand and released the ashes.

I walked around the trees and down to the cliffside trail. Morning was upon me.

I could feel something lifted from my heart as I walked the trail. The summer ran through my mind in mixed-up pieces of pain, joy, salt, and sand. I breathed in the ocean and closed my eyes. I could hear the waves crashing on the rocks. This time they were saying good-bye.

The ocean remained in its constancy.

I knew if I ever returned, it would be here, waiting, like an old friend.

I walked the trail, all the way to the peace sign. I was going to add letters to the big painted boulder where four-year-old Hunter had his initials. A word to encapsulate my summer. One letter at a time.

T. With a black permanent marker, I made small capital letters. I put the first one up near the top and the next letter far from it, off to the left.

R. I didn't put the letters in order or make them big.

U. I just let them blend in with all the other tags. I buried the letters of my word next to the initials of others. No one would find my word. But I would know it was there.

T. I was going to make a promise to myself.

H. To the never-ending sea. A promise that I could feel rising up in me like it had been there all along, but now it was finally bubbling to the surface, freed.

ACKNOWLEDGMENTS

I am so indebted to the amazing and thoughtful work of literary agent extraordinaire George Nicholson and Erica Silverman of Sterling Lord Literistic. Thank you so very much for representing me.

Thanks also to my dear friends who have encouraged me to not give up on this writing journey: Jennifer Mitchell Martin, Joe Scordato, Cindi Jensen, Robin Brooks, Sarah Chaffee Paris, and Catherine Maletz. Thank you to Travis and Christy Bistrek, for their friendship and support (and aid in the cover photography of the original printing of this book!); and thanks to The Salasin Center programs and to early readers, like Loranna Almeida and Amy Pettapiece Morris. Many props go out to Eric and Sandra Lucentini and Mike and Sharanya Mitchell, for sharing great NYC spaces for writing retreats.

ABOUT THE AUTHOR

Emily Stone began her writing career as a newspaper reporter for *The Lewisboro Ledger* in New York and *The Redding Pilot* in Connecticut. Her poetry and prose have been published in the *Boston Globe*. She received a Master of Fine Arts in Creative Writing from Emerson College and a Bachelor of Arts in English from Keene State College.

Emily Stone lives in a sweet little town in New England that has a river running through it and no stoplights. In her spare time, she practices hot yoga, pretends to cook well, and envies her cat's nap-centered lifestyle.

For more info, go to emilystonebooks.com

www.ingramcontent.com/pod-product-compliance
Lightning Source LLC
Chambersburg PA
CBHW030037070525
26304CB00008B/93